Blanche Willis Howard

Tony, the Maid

Blanche Willis Howard

Tony, the Maid

ISBN/EAN: 9783337025717

Printed in Europe, USA, Canada, Australia, Japan

Cover: Foto ©Andreas Hilbeck / pixelio.de

More available books at **www.hansebooks.com**

TONY, THE MAID

A Novelette

BY

BLANCHE WILLIS HOWARD

AUTHOR OF "ONE SUMMER" "GUENN" ETC.

ILLUSTRATED

Ad bonam finem recta omnis via

NEW YORK
HARPER & BROTHERS, FRANKLIN SQUARE

CONTENTS.

ILLUSTRATIONS.

TONY, THE MAID.

CHAPTER I.

MISTRESS AND MAID MEET.

To this day Miss Aurelia Vanderpool does not know exactly what happened, it was all so very sudden. Then Tony never explained. The episode, as related by Miss Aurelia to her Uncle John, in her habitually flurried but conscientious manner, was approximately as follows:

She was coming up from the reading-room at half-past ten that morning. That is, she thought that it was about half-past ten; but it might have been a very little less, say twenty-six or twenty-seven minutes past.

At this point Uncle John began to fidget on his chair, whereupon Miss Aurelia hurriedly resumed her main narrative.

She was coming up, and in the corridor she had been speaking with the head-waiter, who was always so civil, and had such distinguished manners, like a diplomatic person—didn't Uncle John think so?—and they were discussing whether the cloud over Pilatus did or did not mean rain, which led her to consider, as she came up the stairs, whether she should or should not change her shoes; and, to the best of her recollection, she hadn't another idea in her head.

Uncle John's face expressed unflattering confidence in the accuracy of this last statement.

When, suddenly, the door of the corner room on the right burst open, and she saw—what she saw she could not exactly say—and heard—what she heard she felt equally unable to affirm, for she should be grieved, indeed, to do any one, even a perfect stranger, injustice, and she could not reconcile it with her conscience to relate as a fact what the suddenness and her surprise might have caused her to completely misinterpret; and Uncle John knew that anything sudden was apt to confuse her, and to produce too powerful an impression for—

Here Mr. John Vanderpool rattled his newspaper, and interposed,

"Never mind your conscience, Aurelia. Just tell your story, can't you? The facts, my dear, the facts."

She sighed profoundly.

"That is the trouble, uncle; I am not sure that they are facts."

"Well, then, the probable, possible, to be taken with all caution—highest attenuation of the facts."

With an air of abject self-reproach she continued:

"I had just reached the landing when the door opposite flew open, and there was the countess, uncle, looking more corpulent and loosely put together than ever, in a white wrapper or a toilet-sacque—it was all so sudden, I cannot say which—but this I know, positively, Uncle John, it was trimmed with Cluny; and it was big and white and loose and flying in every direction; and she exclaimed something in German too fast for me to understand; at least, that is my impression; and she had a great ivory hairbrush in her upraised hand, and stood between me and the light; and, oh, uncle, there was a movement and there was a sound, and the little maid came spinning—I think I may literally say spinning—over the threshold; and the door slammed, and the little maid picked herself up; she had been flung or pushed or had fallen on one knee; and there I stood and looked at her, and there she stood and looked at me."

Miss Aurelia paused, overcome with horror and her struggle with her conscience.

".Bravo, Aurelia! Go on, go on!"

"How can you laugh, uncle?" she gasped. "It is so terrible!"

"My dear," rejoined Mr. Vanderpool, unfeelingly, "it is the only interesting thing I have ever known to happen in Lucerne. Your impressions are perfect. What next?"

She gave him a pathetic look, as if she were being led sadly astray, and went on, mournfully, ·

"As soon as I had recovered my presence of mind—for, indeed, uncle, whatever the circumstances really may have been, I felt as if the skies had fallen—I said to the little maid, 'Are you hurt? Can I do anything for you?' I suppose I looked agitated."

"I presume there can be no reasonable doubt of that, my dear."

"At all events, the little maid—the whole side of her face was red, uncle—answered me in her nice, cheery, civil, comforting little way, as if nothing unusual had happened—and that is what makes me feel almost as if I had imag-

ined it all, Uncle John, and as if that dishevelled, angry creature, in voluminous, loose rai-
ment, were but a kind of dreadful vision—and
the little maid said, would I please excuse her
for stumbling so awkwardly and startling me.
Then she found my key, which, owing to my
excitement, I had lost, and picked up my handkerchief, which I had accidentally dropped, and
also my eyeglasses, which had fallen, and opened
my door for me, and led me to the sofa, and
poured out a glass of water, and I drank it, and
felt better, her manner was so exceedingly sym-
pathetic and trustworthy. But why you laugh,
uncle, I cannot imagine. Surely the whole affair is most painful, and not in the least funny."

"And then?" he asked, with a chuckle.

"And then she left me, and I read Matthew
Arnold to compose my nerves. An hour later
she came back, and asked me, in the most natural way in the world, if I didn't want a maid.
And that is what I wished to say to you, Uncle
John. Of course, it is very, very sudden, and
requires a great deal of careful thought, and I
impressed it upon her that it was impossible for
me to consider it for an instant until I had con-
sulted you; and I begged her to fully understand that she was to build no real hopes upon

the probability; still I have resolved to go as far
as this—that is to say, if you see no objection—
I should like to try her, Uncle John; I really
think I should."

He gazed meditatively at his niece, whose
whole gentle being seemed to quiver with a
kind of latent apology to the whole world for
the mistake she had made, for the mistake
which she feared she was about to make;
above all, abject apology to her own insatiable
conscience, which tyrannized over her innocent
life with Juggernaut rapacity.

"I wonder that we have never thought of
this before. I wonder that we have waited for
a maid to be literally flung at your head. Why,
if you had one, I could leave you with a clear
conscience."

"Then you really wouldn't mind?"

"Mind? Bless my soul, if the girl is a decent
and honest body I shall receive her with open
arms. Figuratively, my dear, figuratively. The
truth is, Aurelia, Lucerne will be the death of
me soon. There's absolutely nothing for a man
to do in Lucerne but to increase in body and
decrease in mind. I believe I've gained three
quarters of an inch since last week." Mr. Vanderpool looked ruefully at his waistcoat. "I

don't pretend to know why being bored should
make a man stout, but staring at that mori-
bund fossil of a lion has always had that effect
upon me. At all events, the sooner I'm off for
Marienbad the better. And I advise you to
stay here and look at the lion as long as you
like, Aurelia. You, at least, are not threat-
ened with apoplexy."

"I have thought that I should like to go to
Constance a little later, uncle. I've heard it
was so pleasant and quiet."

"Quieter than Lucerne?" he returned, with a
groan. "Well, never mind. Go where you like.
The maid is a good idea, a capital idea. If she's
an honest girl, nothing could be better. What's
her name, by the way?"

Miss Aurelia fluttered with pleasure at his interest in her scheme.

"Antoninia," she replied.

Again he threw back his head and laughed.

"It seems to be a very good name," she remarked deprecatingly, perplexed by his mirth.

"Excellent, excellent. But isn't it too grand
for common use? It's such a mouthful, you
know. Then the two of you together—Aurelia
and Antoninia! Isn't it too imposing for the
way we travel? Doesn't it suggest triumphal
processions and an S.P.Q.R. pomp?"

Miss Aurelia looked at him in mild and distant interrogation.

"Her other name," she continued, seriously, "is Zschorcher. I am not sure that I pronounce that name very well. There's a certain sound I don't seem to get. The German consonants are so difficult. And if I were obliged to say it rapidly, without preparing my mouth for it, I fear I should not do it justice. Zsch—Zschor—Zschorcher."

"As you pronounce it," remarked Uncle John, "it sounds uncommonly like a sneeze."

"If it wouldn't hurt her feelings, we might change it to Bates or Briggs. How would Briggs do, Uncle John? It does not really matter what one calls them, does it, provided they themselves are willing?"

"Well, no, not much, I should say. Still, it's a pity to sacrifice a name that revels in possibilities, like Antoninia. Let her come in, and I'll tell you in a twinkling what to call her. Christening ladies'-maids may not be a suitable occupation for a bachelor of my years, but it's more enlivening than staring at the fossil."

"Oh, uncle!" exclaimed Miss Aurelia.

"Or yawning at the peaks."

"Why, uncle!"

"Or dawdling about the pond."

"The pond! Oh, Uncle John!"

"Or asking head-waiters to interpret the portents of clouds hovering over Pilatus. Great heavens, are waiters augurs? More likely screws. Then, I confess it, Aurelia, I am in mortal dread of Wilhelm Tell."

"Of whom, dear uncle? I do not really understand."

"Of Wilhelm Tell, I say."

"But, uncle—"

"Oh, I don't mean the hero and patriot. He's an egregious bore, but one can escape from him. My Wilhelm is alive. My Wilhelm is not traditionary. You see, I was walking the other day towards Brunnen, with no intentions under heaven except to get away from that beastly lion. On the road I met a woman with a beautiful boy three years old. He was a sturdy, rosy little. chap, with yellow curls and a jolly smile. The fact is, he smiled pointedly at me. He began the mischief himself. I, like an old fool, patted his head. Now, I'm the last man in the world to go about patting children. When did I ever pose for the benevolent old gentleman? But that lion can drive a man into premature senility. Well, I patted him.

Then I said, 'What's your name?' Imbecile question; another result of the lion. The boy only smiled.

"Up spoke the woman. 'Wilhelm Tell,' she said, courtesying.

"'Oh, come now, that's a downright swindle.'

"'No, it isn't,' protested the woman, astonished and aggrieved. 'His father's name is Tell, and this is little Wilhelm.'

"I laughed, gave him a franc, and went my way.

"A few minutes later I heard a voice and hurrying feet behind me.

"It was the honest and indignant woman with her child.

"'Oh, sir,' she began, breathlessly, 'please take little Wilhelm.'

"'Take him!' said I, staring. 'What for?'

"'Take him, and keep him. You may have him.'

"'But I don't want to buy a boy.'

"'You needn't buy him. You may have him for nothing. I have eleven at home. Please take little Wilhelm.'

"'Woman, are you his mother?' I demanded, sternly.

"'Of course I am. That's why I want you to take him. Oh, kind sir, do, do take little Wilhelm.

"Well, Aurelia, to cut a long story short, I broke loose from her that time. Fancy me travelling about with a three-year-old boy, and the charitable remarks in consequence! But I don't trust myself. That lion can lead a man into any folly, any crime. The worst of it is, Wilhelm Tell's mother knows I am weak, and is lying in wait for me. If I don't run away, she'll have me yet. I meet them everywhere, and, unless I wish Wilhelm Tell saddled on me for life, I'd better go."

"But, how beautiful it would be, uncle, how tender, kind, and benevolent!"

"No, my dear, thanks! No merry Swiss boy for me. How do I know what he has inherited? By the time he is fourteen he may develop a goitre; he may be a cretin. The lion must commit further ravages upon my intellect before I recklessly adopt. Still, I confess my weakness. There is safety in flight, for the smile of Wilhelm Tell works like madness in my brain. Who knows? Perhaps he can't do anything but smile. I never heard him say a word. Do you happen to know, Aurelia, if boys of three usually converse?"

"I think that they gently prattle, uncle."

"Gently prattle! H'm! Well, summon your

Roman Abigail, and I'll give her a name con-
structed out of a mere fragment of the one with
which she is so plentifully supplied. And then,
if she seems to be the right kind of a person to
look after you—though, to be sure, you of all
women are safe enough anywhere—"

"Yes," interrupted Miss Aurelia, bridling
softly; "I hope that my dignity, my discretion—"

"Bless my soul, it's no question of dignity
and discretion. Absence of danger doesn't by
any means invariably depend upon high-toned
qualities. Never mind, Aurelia. You are a
very good girl, if we don't always understand
each other."

"It is stupid for you with only me, I know,"
she rejoined, gently. "I wonder that you have
had so much patience. Do start at once for
Marienbad. I am sure that you will like Antoninia. But, Uncle John, I am beginning to
have my misgivings. If this should be too lux-
urious, too self-indulgent? You know I do not
positively require a maid. I have no sewing
whatever at present, except an occasional stitch
in a glove, or something equally trifling. If I
should be yielding to a weak impulse? If the
money which I shall pay Antoninia could be

used to better advantage devoted to the Society for Teaching Indigent Young Women the Use of the Caligraph?"

"Aurelia," interposed her uncle, gravely, "charity begins at home. Have I not remained here three weeks longer than our agreement, waiting for your friends, whom some instinct of self-preservation has led elsewhere? Do you wish to save me from enlargement of the liver and softening of the brain? Do you not perceive the imminent danger of the descent of Wilhelm Tell? Then produce your maid."

"I will, I will," responded Miss Aurelia, agitated but resolute, and rising to ring the bell.

Presently the waiter ushered in a small, dark-haired girl of seven or eight and twenty, who entered with a complete absence of bustle, and stood facing Mr. Vanderpool. Her deep-set, shrewd eyes gazed at him calmly, her firm, small hands were quietly clasped across her white apron, her whole personality expressed repose.

"She'll do," he thought. "Frisky she isn't, or handsome, but wholesome she is, and cleverer than the whole Vanderpool race."

Miss Aurelia's anxious, gentle, helpless glance fluttered from one to the other. The little maid

met her gaze, and returned it with what seemed
to Mr. Vanderpool a very remarkable smile.   It
was deferential in the extreme, yet eminently
reassuring.   It was the smile of a strong and
tender nature protecting a weaker one.   Moreover it was a warm smile, brilliantly lighting
the calm, self-contained face, and displaying two
rows of faultless teeth.

"Upon my word," muttered Mr. Vanderpool,
"she is handsome, in her way."

Grave and demure she watched her judge.

"The girl is spirited; Annie is too tame.
She hasn't an atom of coquetry.   Nina is too
sentimental.   Tony might mean anything, so
might she," reasoned the nomenclator with a
chuckle.   "But if she's a Jesuit she's an honest
one."

"Aurelia," he said, "she's an unknown quan-
tity.   For that matter, so is every woman who
is interesting.   Her certificates are useless, as
we can't hunt up the parties who wrote them
or find somebody to certify to their honesty.
We shall have to risk it."

"But oh, uncle, she looks so conscientious, so
high-principled."

"I don't know how she looks," rejoined Uncle John, dryly.   "I know I never saw any-

body like her. I'll cross-examine her a little if you wish."

"Why did you leave your last place so suddenly?" he began.

"The gracious countess has continued her journey without me."

Her voice was as clear as her gaze, with finished intonations.

"Already?"

"Already. In a landau. To Interlaken," she replied, succinctly.

"I am curious to see how far this wonderful discretion will go," he remarked in English.

"Your gracious countess was a bit of a vixen, wasn't she? Apt to be violent and fling things about now and then? Made it rather hard for you, didn't she? Don't be afraid; you can speak out safely here."

Can any woman resist the satisfaction of hitting an enemy when the enemy can't hit back, he wondered.

"She had a great deal of vivacity," admitted the girl seriously.

"What was she trying to do with that hairbrush?"

A change swept over Antoninia's face. Her straight eyebrows, which always had a slight upward slant, suddenly ran almost to a point above her nose. Her features were alive with keen intelligence, and her eyes, fixed sharply upon Mr. Vanderpool's, seemed to convey from her spirit to his a burden of extraordinary reminiscence. He flattered himself that he possessed as little imagination as any man alive, yet in that illuminated instant he felt that he was gazing upon a long perspective of horrors, beginning that morning at the insulting blow of the irate countess, and leading through unspeakable grievances back to her ancestral racks and thumbscrews, to the dungeons and oubliettes of her high-born, high-tempered race. He was fairly startled. Before he could quite interpret the look it was gone, and the girl's clear voice was replying with precise old-fashioned phrases:

"Knowing my duty—I allow myself to remark to the gracious gentleman that the best of families have their little eccentricities."

"She did have eccentricities, then?" he persisted.

"That is to say," corrected Antoninia Zschorcher, with beautiful deference, "we had differences of opinion."

"Euphuistic for a whack with a hairbrush,"

he muttered. "And what made you apply to Miss Vanderpool?"

She turned her bright face, again radiant with the fine smile, upon the lank figure and uncertain, gentle features of Miss Aurelia.

"If I may be so bold," she began, "I have had the honor of meeting the gracious fräulein in the corridor for several weeks, and I have observed her, and I have thought she looked as if she might need precisely such a person as I" —to take care of her, she did not add, but Mr. Vanderpool supplied it mentally.

"Knowing my duty," she went on cheerfully, "I believe I should suit. I make bold to say that if the gracious fräulein engages me she will have no reason to regret it."

Her self-respect, her command of the situation, the extreme finish of her manner, pleased and puzzled Mr. Vanderpool, while Miss Aurelia was plainly under a spell.

"What shall you do if we don't take you?" he asked.

"I shall start to-day for Germany. I have examined all the ladies in the house. There is none to whom I wish to apply beside the gracious fräulein."

"Aurelia, engage her on the spot, and call

2

her Tony. Lucerne may have undermined my intellect more than I myself am aware, and I may be doing a rash thing; still, I should trust a man that looked like this girl. You can examine her papers for form's sake. If the effete aristocracy of the old world maltreat her, we'll shelter her upon our broad shores," and off he sauntered to stare at the lion for the last time.

"That girl has an air of race," he reflected, as he gazed up at the hated object embedded in the rock. "I don't know where she got it, but it's taken several centuries to produce her."

The next morning, in excellent spirits, he started for Marienbad.

"Good-bye, Aurelia. Take care of yourself. Don't hesitate to telegraph if you need me. You've got a treasure of a maid," chuckled the wicked old gentleman. "She's feudal; she's mediæval. But I'll tell you what, Aurelia, you'll have to live up to her!"

CHAPTER II.

TONY CONVOYS HER MISTRESS TO CONSTANCE.

THE quiet old town of Constance was enlivened a certain season by a feud. In a summer resort whose picturesqueness is characterized by interminable tranquillity, and whose extremest pleasure is the reverse of madly reckless, a feud is obviously a boon. Now any feud, with all its ramifications, is rather a difficult thing to tackle, that is, when one is not born and brought up with it, educated to it, as it were. The travelling public never attempted to grasp the beginning or end of this one, but embraced it on that account with no less fervor. It was a hotel feud and appertained exclusively to the summer guests.

The Constanzer Hof was big, airy, clean, and glaringly modern. The Insel Hôtel was serious, ancient, and picturesque, an old Dominican monastery, forced, at this late period of its existence, to reluctantly serve a frivolous passing throng.

The guests at the Constanzer superciliously wondered that people could deliberately choose to inhabit a place choked by the dust of ages, and permeated by a musty, mouldy, not to say monkish, flavor. The Inselites, conscious of picturesqueness, prowled along dark, stuffy corridors to their rooms, ate their dinners with gusto in the vaulted and dim refectory, and thanked Providence that they were not as their prosaic neighbors in the flagrantly new and monstrous building which desecrated the opposite shore, and was a blot upon the face of nature.

It must be admitted that the prerogative of the Insel devotees entailed upon them certain arduous observances; for instance, an appropriate significance of costume and bearing. One was not always clear in one's own mind exactly how lofty an expression one ought to assume when one happened to be standing by the tanks watching the swans, and a party of fashionable loungers from the Constanzer strolled along. Upon some, the mantle of the defunct friars hung awkwardly enough, but certain æsthetic English maidens wore it with admirable seriousness and ease. On any excursion steamer, in the midst of a giddy pleasure-seeking throng, an observing eye could perceive that they were never unconscious of the subtle Dominican influence brooding over them; and sometimes, on a lonely hill-top, one would meet a damsel who wore her colors as distinctly as if she were a page of illuminated vellum.

The feud created tough and indestructible topics of conversation invaluable in a place where little happened, and that little seldom. People blessed with a partisan spirit had been known to take it so seriously that, coming for two days, they had remained two months; and, far from considering Constance a dead little place, as their friends had described it, they had found its attractions more enlivening than any Alpine panorama they had seen.

Down in his den below the summer-idlers, sat a serious-minded man, and every evening, with the sphinx-like, fateful smile of the hotel-keeper, he lumped the payments of the æsthetes and the worldlings. Over the weal and woe of both houses presided one and the same power. He created and encouraged the rivalry. He sowed, and, most especially, he reaped. Any hotel can have an elevator, he reasoned. Not every one may boast an artistic feud. So he pulled his wires, and the puppets merrily danced.

Antoninia Zschorcher was nobody's puppet.

Whatever terpsichorean or other exercise she undertook was apt to be at the instigation of her own spirit. When she and Miss Aurelia stood on the platform of the railway station at Constance, she was ignorant of the place and all its works. But at such moments she usually proceeded upon certain broad general principles. Miss Aurelia, never in the thirty-three years of her existence so advantageously dressed, and already feeling safe under Tony's convoy, waited with a passive and amiable expression of countenance until the master mind should act.

Tony looked sharply about, and inspected the line of omnibuses drawn up to receive the victims. She perceived that two large hotels and several inns were represented, and caught the exchange of a knowing wink between two portly blond men who stood apparently glowering fiercely at each other at the doors of the Constanzer Hof and Insel Hôtel vehicles, into which they were abstractedly pushing women and bundles. The Insel man was the nearer. Miss Aurelia admired his gold stripes, and thought that he looked like a major-general. With the vivacity of a squirrel little Tony darted towards this imposing personage, and slipped a silver coin into his largely receptive hand.

"Which is the cleaner?" she demanded.

He gave her a glance of recognition, not of the individual, but of the type.

"II'm," he returned, grinning. "Got anybody in particular?"

"Yes, yes. Hurry, can't you? Which is the cleaner and the best table?"

"The other one," he muttered; "but it's all the same thing, you know."

"Thank you, kindly," she said, nodding and smiling. "I'll do as much for you some day."

The gong at the Constanzer Hof portals announced the approach of the omnibus which disgorged that evening an endless stream of warm and weary beings, each of whom, very naturally, wished to be treated a little better than anybody else. Breathless, hungry-looking waiters skimmed and circled about the guests like a covey of black, gaunt birds. To the babel of bad German and French the hotel director added his pleasingly bad English, each individual being apparently determined to avail himself exclusively of the language with which he was least acquainted. Smiling, suave—a striking example of the triumph of mind over matter—the director stood heroically in the centre of the heterogeneous surging mass of men, women, travelling - bags, shawl - straps, and umbrellas. His hair may have been slightly dishevelled, his eye a trifle wild, but his voice never faltered as he gave the most encouraging acquiescence to the universal demand for first-floor rooms at fifth-floor prices, and windows with a southern exposure and adapted to seeing the sunset, on the northeast shady side. '

"Your pleasantest corner room for a single lady," said a clear tone at his elbow. He turned and saw a decided little person with an eye that meant business.

"Who is it?" he asked, also recognizing Tony's type. His pallid features expressed sudden relief, and the artificial strained Swiss honey vanished from his smile.

"Miss Vanderpool," replied Tony, enunciating the name with ineffable respect. •

He raised his eyebrows and searched his memory.

" *The* Vanderpool family," she added, coming easily to his aid.

"Oh, ah, yes, yes, of course," he returned, vaguely, but with deference.

"It's worth your while to please her, you know," she murmured, confidentially, "in every way," she added with significance. "Give her something good, and put me anywhere you like, but near her."

"Henri!" the director beckoned to one of the black-coated phantoms, "show this lady to 53."

The waiter stared and ventured to remind his chief:

"Reserved for the Princess Shilly-Shally."

"53 for the lady," repeated the autocrat.

Henri swooped down upon Miss Aurelia's travelling accoutrements and ascended the great stairway like a perambulating Colossus of Rhodes.

Presently Miss Aurelia found herself in a large arm-chair by a window overlooking the garden and lake, and waited upon, watched over, and protected like a cradled infant. She had not elected to join the worldlings, was not cognizant of the existence of the æsthetes, and did not dream that she had made her entry with banners flying and had even ousted a princess. It was the first time in her life that she had been thoroughly taken care of, and she felt exceedingly comfortable and happy. Accustomed to a patronizing masculine protection, to the careless good-nature of a superior being to whom she helplessly clung, sensitive to his approbation

and painfully conscious that she rarely gained
it, wincing daily beneath the covert irony of his
bluff tolerance, her enjoyment of Tony would
be difficult to portray. Uncle John was good
to her, often patient, always generous; but the
fact remained, his niece was a persistently humorous object to him, and this she vaguely but
sorely felt.

The balminess, then, of two weeks of Tony
transcended a cycle of Uncle John. The deli-
ciousness of being approached with deference,
handled with care; the luxury of having her
judgment gravely solicited; in short, the bliss of
being important—all this was novel and sweet to
Miss Aurelia's much-repressed being. But Tony
was so bonny and bright, so quick and clever, so
superior, so near perfection, her mistress might
have been overawed in spite of the maid's gentle and respectful demeanor, were it not for one
fortunate flaw, one comforting suggestion of in-
competency. Apparently Tony did not know
right from left; at least, when she brought Miss
Aurelia's slippers, she invariably, after removing
her mistress's boots, applied the left slipper to
the right foot.

"Do you not see, Tony," Miss Aurelia would
say, instructively, "even in well-formed feet"

—she was a little vain of her foot, considering it slender and aristocratic—"there must be a difference, there is always the mark of the great toe. Right and left — that is so easy, Tony, if you only think."

"When the gracious fräulein explains it so nicely, I seem to understand,". Tony would reply, kneeling before her; "but, alas! I must be incurable, since I always commit the same fault."

She did, indeed. Regularly every evening, at the hour of changing shoes, the inexplicable mistake reoccurred. Her brilliant smile, handsome teeth, and the benevolent dimple in her chin lost none of their cheerfulness during Miss Aurelia's gently didactic disquisition upon the formation of the human foot. But the necessity of giving it imparted each day strength and dignity to that lady's position, as mistress of this all but faultless maid; and when she closed her eyes to sleep, after her anatomical lecture, it was with a feeling of solid self-respect, such as she had never before known.

And Tony? In flat contradiction to the misanthropic old saw, "No man is a hero to his valet," her stanch heart required nothing less than a heroine for a mistress. She would have

economically created one for herself anywhere
out of the most minute heroic fragments, and
no money could have induced her to remain
long in a situation untenable for hero-worship.
The prevailing conditions of her last engagement were, as has been indicated, turbulent.
She had her own immutable code, and volunta-
rily closed her eyes to many idiosyncrasies of
her previous mistress. "Why have we eyes
that open and shut, unless we are sometimes to
shut them," reasoned Tony. Tyranny and ca-
price disturbed her little. According to her
broad philosophy a lady could be tyrannical and
capricious to her heart's content, provided she
would observe proper forms. This the fair
countess emphatically refused to do, and Tony,
in consequence, left her, but not before her ex-
alted sense of decorum had been subjected to a
series of great and frequent shocks. She suffered more in spirit from the disorderly relation-
ship of mistress and maid than physically from
what may be politely termed accidental concus-
sions. Her soul loathed disorder. Her boxes
and drawers were marvels of symmetrical layers,
and bundles bound with blue ribbons tied in
prim little bows; her ideas, too, were assort-
ed in the neatest manner, all their folds and

"WHEN THE GRACIOUS FRAULEIN EXPLAINS IT SO NICELY."

frills held within exact bounds, and bearing the prim little sign-manual of their owner.

When Tony took Miss Aurelia under her protection, that is to say, when in the eyes of the world Tony entered Miss Aurelia's service, she took her for better for worse, and elevated her on the spot to heroship. She laid at her feet the accumulated homage which she had been forced to withdraw from the countess, and much beside that arose from ardent gratitude. Attaching herself speedily to the mild and somewhat helpless lady, she served her according to her lights. It is by no means asserted that Tony's were the best lights in the world, but, such as they were, they burned clear and strong, and were always ready for use, like the lamps of the wise virgins. Miss Aurelia's tremulous hesitation, her apologetic softness, seemed plaintive to cheery little Tony, trained to bear with patience the immeasurable exactions of another order of woman; and anything this side of the kingdom of heaven more restful than Miss Aurelia's service it was not in the power of Tony's imagination to picture.

The evening of their arrival in Constance, having deposited her mistress in the easy-chair by the pleasant window and quickly unpacked

a dressing-case, Tony proposed to bring a slight
refreshment of which Miss Aurelia could par-
take while enjoying the view.

"Or I could go down myself, Tony, and see
if, by chance, anybody I know is here."

"The gracious fräulein could, indeed, if she
were not already so fatigued, and here it is quiet and cool, and the gracious fräulein can be so
comfortable, while down-stairs it is noisy with
many new arrivals."

"That is true, Tony. You might bring me
a cup of tea, here."

"Or a half bottle of wine?"

Tony approved of wine, and was prejudiced
against tea.

"And you could give me my embroidery as I
sit here."

"Or the pleasant book which amuses the gracious fräulein so much," suggested Tony, with
her convincing smile. She thought Miss Aurelia stooped too much over her needlework.

Miss Aurelia turned, and looked meditatively
out of the window.

Tony waited, motionless.

"Tony," at length began Miss Aurelia, with
a gentle dignity born of the conditions which
for two weeks had beautified and enlarged her

life, "as I am already somewhat fatigued, and
it is quiet and cool and comfortable here, and so
very noisy down-stairs with all the arrivals, you
may bring me some lunch and a little wine, and,
Tony, give me the Tauchnitz volume I was reading on the train, please."

Tony gravely obeyed.

Mutually satisfied, mistress and maid sepa-
rated.

Tony now descended to the lower regions to
take bearings, and discover as soon as possible
that most important guide to conduct above and
below stairs—in which direction salaams must be
made. Meeting three yawning waiters cumber-
ing the passage, she sent one of them flying for
fresher than fresh water, another for a rose from
the garden, and the third to find a salver of a
special shape and size. In consequence, as she
entered the servants' dining-room, she was short-
ly followed by her vassals.

The room was large and comfortable. At a
small table sat a heavy, elderly, red-faced man
solemnly drinking beer. Tony with one glance
took his mental measure.. Only a gentleman's
gentleman could attain to that expression of co-
lossal arrogance when exclusively enjoying his
own society. Through a succession of open

doors an agreeable kitchen perspective was visible, and a handsome, white-capped French cook
at the head of his minions and scullions. Tony,
with great ingenuity, kept the three waiters
ministering to her wants. The salver was not
quite to her taste, the napkin was not folded
properly, the bread was too old, the wine too
new. But her smile and her voice compensated
for her exactions. The great man drinking beer
turned his somewhat glassy eyes upon her.
Tony, having nearly completed her arrange-
ments, stepped back and regarded the tray crit-
ically. The three lank waiters watched her
open-mouthed. The great man put down his
beer-glass and stared. Tony walked by him
with composure, and passed through the room
and adjoining pantries straight into the kitchen,
where she accosted the *cordon bleu* in his own
language. The Frenchman was a gallant man,
and liked cheery little maids with neat waists
and bright eyes. To her practical inquiry if he
had not something nice to tempt her lady's appetite, he generously responded by displaying a
series of choicest tidbits, begged her to apply
to him personally every day, and assured her he
and his larder were at her feet.

Tony, always simple and modest before true

merit, gratefully replied that she should deeply
regret giving him the slightest trouble, but he
would readily understand that for a lady like
her lady, Miss Vanderpool, nothing in this im-
perfect world could be too good.

The Frenchman responded that her sentiments
were most elevated, and she could rely upon
him.   In fact, he would at once dedicate a re-
cent creation of his genius, a brilliant composi-
tion for which he sought a fitting name, to her
lady.   On the next day's *menu* she would perceive "*Poudding à la Vanderpool.*"   He escorted her to the entrance of his realm, where they
parted with delightful ceremony and expressions
of mutual esteem.

This episode was closely observed by the great
man with the beer.   "Who in the dickens is
this genteel little body that walks calmly over
the course, and exerts influence in high places?"
he asked himself.   For, after all, to a truly
thoughtful observer, the greatest man in a great
hotel is the *cordon bleu.*

Preceded by a waiter to open doors, followed
by a waiter with the tray, and with waiters bow-
ing obsequiously as she passed, Tony made her
exit.   The gentleman's gentleman in the corner,
accustomed, like all great persons, to be fawned

3

upon, was unconsciously impressed by the indifference with which she had treated him. When, after ten or fifteen minutes, having ministered to the needs of her mistress, she returned and seated herself with a fine air of leisure, he was pleasurably moved.

"Anything will do for me," she said to a waiter, with amiable negligence. "A little bread and meat and a glass of wine." This was all that had been served to her mistress; but everything in this world depends upon the point of view.

"I should conclude," mused the great man in the corner, "that she had nothing less than a duchess in tow."

Waiting for her modest repast, Tony gazed into space with an expression of refined insolence. It was the one thing which she had chosen to learn from the countess, and it sat better on the maid than on the lady of high degree; for Tony's face was fine, with a delicate, slightly aquiline nose, and sensitive curves playing about the mouth, and a cheerfully satirical gleam of the eye, while the countess, viewed in the most charitable light, was but a somewhat shapeless mass of humanity.

The grand mogul coughed and deigned to draw near.

"HE ESCORTED HER TO THE ENTRANCE OF HIS REALM."

"Ahem!" he said. "You are new, I believe."

Tony had deftly extracted from the waiters, as they journeyed up-stairs, all that it was important to know about "permanents." She therefore smiled her prettiest with that frank deference far removed from servility, supposed to be pleasing to clever sovereigns, and answered, sweetly,

"We have just arrived."

"H'm," he returned, regarding her neat little person with an approving stare, then relapsed into silence.

"So glad to find genteel society," chirped Tony.

"Passable, passable," he returned, gloomily. "Unfortunately there's always considerable second-class that travels."

"There is," sighed Tony, responsively depressed.

"Why second-class folks travel at all is a mystery," he continued. "It would be better taste if such as they should just stay modestly at home, and not intrude themselves on such as we."

"It would, indeed," echoed Tony, resolutely pulling down the corners of her mouth, over which her eyes were twinkling rebelliously;

"but, dear, dear," she added, with the countess's own stare, "what can one expect of *them?*"

"True, too true," he groaned. He then regarded her with a searching look, as if to satisfy himself that he was not about to impart a sacred mystery to an unworthy being, or a scoffer.

"We," he announced, with immeasurable loftiness, "we are the High-Dudgeons."

"And we," returned Tony, equally superb, "we are—the Vanderpools."

She filled her glass with red wine, and cut a slice of bread from the narrow French loaf with an abstracted air.

"Vanderpool?" repeated the great man, slowly and interrogatively.

"My last engagement," she communicated, frankly, "was with the Countess Blaublutheim."

"I know that family," said the man, quickly.

"I don't say that it isn't a very good family," she continued, balancing her fork, reflectively; "but there are better," smiling triumphantly at her new acquaintance.

"It's a well-known family," he ventured to say.

"Oh dear, yes," she responded, indifferently; "but the tone left something to be desired. Tone, tone, it is a necessity of my being!"

"Ah!" he murmured, expansively, "I was sure the instant I saw you that you were one of us. Vanderpool is the name?"

"Vanderpool. The Vanderpools."

Not to know Vanderpool argued himself unknown was the eloquent burden of Tony's speech.

"Good-evening, Mr.—"

"High-Dudgeon," prompted the great man, majestically. "General High-Dudgeon. *Major*-General."

Tony, having travelled far and wide, at once perceived that she was in a hotel where the second table enjoyed a special distinction; where its society represented in small the claims of its masters; and where, to avoid commonplace repetitions of Marie and Thomas, and to spare overcharged memories the trouble of learning surnames, people were designated, with elegant simplicity, by the appellations of the families which had the honor of employing them.

"Good-evening, major-general. Best thanks," she returned, with her lowest courtesy.

"Good-evening, Miss Vanderpool," he reciprocated, highly pleased.

Late that night, in her stuffy little room which opened upon the square court in the in-

terior of the vast building, and which smelt of
the ghosts of long-perished dinners, Tony, by
the flickering light of a tallow dip, wrote a long
letter. She addressed it, in a singularly masculine hand for a German girl, to Herr Eduard
Maler, in a certain little town of the Suabian
Oberland. As she wrote, her cleanly-cut mouth
curved in innumerable smiles over her pretty
teeth, and her whole expression hovered on the
borderland between roguishness and malice.
She said her prayers scrupulously, after the Roman Catholic form; but the smile on her lips
and in her dancing, rebellious eyes, lingered
through all her observances. Tony found the
world amusing. She looked across the corridor,
where all was silent in Miss Aurelia's virgin
bower. By the dim light Tony perceived two
long and slender boots, turned up slightly at the
toes, indicating a low instep and an uncertain
tread. She took them up, and conscientiously
inspected the condition of their buttons.

"Right—left," she murmured, smiling, and in
the smile was now no malice, only warmth and
infinite protection. "Right—left; it is so easy,
Tony, if you think," she repeated softly, putting the boots back against the door.

"The dear, good, innocent lady!"

CHAPTER III.

It would scarcely be overpraise to state that Tony's method of presenting Miss Aurelia to the distinguished consideration of the hotel world of Constance bore a certain resemblance to the tactics of that perfect herald and astute observer of men, Puss-in-Boots, announcing along the highway the approach of the Marquis of Carabas. She did not create her surroundings. She simply adapted herself to them. She lived in no ideal world, and was unacquainted with the atmosphere of the moon. Hard experience had taught her to call a spade a spade in her own inner consciousness. What name she gave the homely implement before the world varied with circumstances.

Not so much what she said as what she did not say produced a subtle and powerful impression. She seemed always to rely upon the in-

telligence of her auditors to supply what discretion forbade her to reveal. She never,
for instance, stated that Miss Aurelia was the
descendant of a duke, never boasted that she
owned a couple of silver mines; but when dukes
and silver mines and such pleasing trifles were
under discussion in the servants' hall, Tony's
face wore an expression of impenetrable reserve
and sagacity. She became conspicuously inat-
tentive when others were thrilled with curiosity. She yawned politely behind her hand
at tales of magnificence which amazed her col-
leagues. Then her devotion, her haste, her important air when performing the smallest duty
for Miss Aurelia was in itself eloquent. "Only a
shawl, it is true," her zeal seemed to say; "but,
consider—Miss Vanderpool's shawl! It is merely a glass of water, but, oh, fellow-citizens of
Vanity Fair, do you not perceive? it is Miss
Vanderpool's glass of water."

In the genial society of the servants' dining-
room, Tony occupied before twenty-four hours
had passed an enviably secure position, and
even graced at dinner the seat of honor at the
general's right hand.

The general, at this time, deigning to officiate
in the capacity of valet to a modest and infirm

old gentleman, a retired officer of the English army, remarked to a friend, who happened to be travelling with the Ruy-Bric family,

"I say, Ruy-Bric, little Vanderpool's got a prize. One of them deuced Hamerican million-airesses, you know."

"What luck!" sighed the other. "As for me, I strikes family—always family. We are connected by marriage with the Sadflints, you know. It's a bottomless pit of family. But in all my experience I never hit upon anything substantial, never hear the cheerful chink of the coin!"

"Fam'ly is fam'ly," returned High-Dudgeon.

"I don't say it ain't," his colleague rejoined, disconsolately, "and when it's all you've got you'd better make the most of it. But since you've seen so much of it on the market dirt cheap you can't feel as you used to about it. Family! you can buy all you want anywhere. Once you couldn't. Once it was all genuine— your old carved oak, your lozenge panes, your 'scutcheon. But now, when you can buy up a good old name, and even put another pearl on your coronet, and nobody's astonished, or grins, except behind your back, why, all I have to say is, family's a drug in the market."

"Ruy-Bric," said his friend, sternly, "somebody's been corruptin' your morals. For a man of your genteel hassociations such parvenoo feelin's is nothin' less than sinful."

"Well, well, general, I was only letting myself out to you."

"Don't let me hear you do it again. I heard a promisin' young man like you talk so once, but he came to a bad end. What with the flighty Frenchmen an' Hitalian adventurers and most uncertain Germans, who is to keep up the tone of this society if it ain't you and me? Stick to fam'ly, Ruy-Bric. It's safest in the long run. Don't fly in the face of Providence. It's too painful to listen to you."

"You're right, High-Dudgeon, and I'm obliged to you for your warning."

The two shook hands feelingly.

"Well, as I was sayin', Vanderpool's got a prize. Her lady owns mines, railways, cities—could buy up half of Europe; but mind you, Ruy-Bric, she's got fam'ly, too, otherwise, I, for one, shouldn't notice her."

"Did little Vanderpool tell you?"

"Not she. She's truly first-class. Only parvenoos tells. I gathered it, Ruy-Bric. A man like me gathers."

Ruy-Bric gave his oracular friend a farewell glance of admiration, and departed to disseminate the news.

It spread and multiplied as a grain of mustard seed. By that night, when Miss Aurelia modestly passed through the corridor, all the stray valets and couriers and ladies-maids inclined themselves as before a princess travelling incognito. As a natural consequence, by the next noon, all the masters and mistresses of the phalanx of valets, etc., regarded the unknown and unconscious Miss Aurelia as an important factor in their calculations.

Momentary opposition only made Tony's claims surer and safer. A transient and light-minded Frenchman, answering to the name of the Baron, and wearing an insolent little imperial, suddenly appeared in that select and sedate circle below stairs, where Britannic ideas prevailed. Turning towards Tony, before the whole assembly, he remarked, superciliously,

"Vanderpool? The name is not in the 'Almanach de Gotha.' We never travel without one, and I looked."

Not one of the honored names represented at that convivial board happened to adorn the Gotha almanac. The more reason why every eye should now glare accusingly at Tony.

"A gentleman of your education, baron," she replied, with the composure of an easy conscience, "is undoubtedly aware that we have a different almanac in America. We, too, always travel with ours, and our name is in it."

This was strictly true. Tony had seen Miss Aurelia repeatedly take from her portfolio a yellow pamphlet, upon whose fly-leaf Aurelia Vanderpool was written in lead-pencil, and upon whose back "Ayer's Cherry Pectoral" shone out in commanding characters.

"Of course," coughed the baron, with some embarrassment. "America is a great country."

"Oh dear, yes," returned Tony, tranquilly.

In spite of her urbanity, the baron felt vaguely conscious of being defrauded, and after some moments returned to the charge.

"Vanderpool? But which Vanderpool? what Vanderpool?" he demanded.

"What Vanderpool?" repeated the chorus, with stony stares.

Tony put down her knife and fork. There was a pause, which she employed in shrugging her shoulders, raising her eyebrows, and expressing other signs of commiseration. One must have patience, even with gross ignorance, her pantomime said. She gave the general a long look, and waited. It was a happy moment. He had just finished his third bottle of ale, and more solemnly significant than he no owl could appear.

Vaguely aware that something was incumbent upon him, in response to Tony's magnetic appeal he ejaculated huskily:

" *The* Vanderpool!" his heavy eyes blinking slowly upon his subjects.

' What more was needed? The chorus now stared instructively at the baron, who, in order to reinstate himself in public opinion, could do no less than hasten to observe:

" Ah, indeed! Well, I rather suspected as much from the first."

He repented his rashness, but realized that he could never maintain his legitimate position at that table. Accordingly he influenced the young gentleman whose privilege it was to be his companion on this summer tour to leave the hotel the next day. The two became zealous Inselites.

After this episode, which teaches us, among other things, how important it is to travel with our credentials, no valet who respected himself could afford to be ignorant of Miss Aurelia's social position. "Permanents" and "transients"

delighted to honor her. Everywhere she appeared she met with profound bows, long and
respectful looks. The director, with whomever
he might be speaking, turned, and as it were presented arms when she passed. There was a
palpable stir of interest when she entered the
dining-hall. And if the wheat sheaves in the
summer fields had made their obeisance to her
it would not have surprised the hotel folk, still
less Miss Aurelia herself. For modest and
gentle as she was, she had accustomed herself
with surprising rapidity to the new atmosphere. Every night she recorded in her diary
that everybody was so nice and amiable and civil
it was a pleasure to live. She enjoyed being a
person of distinction, and drank in adulation as
a flower drinketh dew.

Meanwhile, she had not yet made her appearance in the drawing-room. Why, she did not
know. It had happened so. Something had
detained her every evening in her own room.
Either she had just returned, a little tired, from
a walk, and Tony put her into her wrapper and
slippers and made her so comfortable that she
had no wish to go down-stairs among strangers;
or there was something to try on, for Miss
Aurelia's wardrobe, like her spirit, was expand-

ing marvellously under Tony's skilful manipulation; or Tony brought her the freshest Tauchnitz volume, or related some long experience which not only hugely entertained her mistress, but also increased that lady's knowledge of German, and Miss Aurelia considered it a duty to make progress in foreign languages. Whatever was the cause, Miss Vanderpool, for some days after her arrival, produced in the house an impression of extreme reserve and complete indifference to her fellow-lodgers. This enhanced her value, and increased their curiosity and respect.

In the ladies' drawing-room, where, on the vast expanse of shining floor, small and isolated groups—like a kind of human archipelago—gathered evenings with needlework and looked askance at one another, Mrs. High - Dudgeon reigned supreme, the central figure of the most austerely aristocratic circle. She was a short, stout woman of an irate expression of countenance, somewhat like the Red Queen in Alice. Whether with or without reason, she gave one the impression that her clothes were too tight, and this supposition seemed to be the most charitable explanation of her chronic irritability. She was usually arrayed in a thick, reddish-pur-

ple satin, which creaked and lent a dusky glow
to her complexion. When a new name was
mentioned in her hearing she invariably sniffed
and snorted in a belligerent manner, and with a
harsh and husky voice and reverberating final
emphasis, demanded,

" Is she a *lady ?*"

Mrs. High-Dudgeon had spent several succes-
sive summers at Constance. As no one by any
accident had ever summoned her before the tri-
bunal of her own scathing inquiry, her pre-emi-
nence had never been disputed. Surrounded by
her satellites, a piece of canvas in her hand, she
entered the drawing-room every evening at a
given hour, and seated herself in a particular
chair, her arms motionless before her like a
Chinese idol's. Her presence was invaluable in
preserving that atmosphere of gloom observable
wherever numerous women are gathered together without introductions.

Nearest to her in the social scale was Mrs.
Ruy-Bric, a grandmother with a neat and light
little juvenile figure, which she arrayed in fashionable toilets from Paris. Her specialties
were religion and family, upon which themes
she conversed exclusively. She was High
Church, so high, indeed, that her spiritual alti-

tude was the plane of eternal ice and snow. Her
boundless devotion to the English curate was a
prominent feature in Constance relationships
that summer. He was a roly-poly little man,
possessed of an inordinate appetite, an unctuous
voice, and, in his corporeal structure, of what
the irreverent called a bow-window. Mrs. Ruy-
Bric sat next him at dinner, and always took a
double portion of pastry and sweets that she
might tenderly convey them to his plate, while
discoursing upon chasubles and stoles. Often,
late at night, they might be seen sitting together
in a corner, communing in low tones.

Mrs. Ruy-Bric never ceased to deplore the laxity of the present chaplain's predecessor, a pale,
sad, lame man, who was devoting the entire
power of his frail body and great soul to a min-
ing population in Lancashire, discovering and
nourishing every germ of good in beings akin to
savages. He had been sent for a few weeks to
Switzerland, and had officiated three Sundays
at Constance, where his earnestness was sadly
out of place.

"Ah, he was Low, dear Mr. Puggums," sighed
Mrs. Ruy-Bric, in the twilight *tête-à-tête*, "ap-
pallingly Low, the very emanations of his mind
were Low!"

4

And Mr. Puggums, "specially appointed by the Bishop of London"—if that dignitary but knew all for which he is responsible in Continental hotels!—nursed his rotund, overfed figure with the complacency of a fetich, and gasped asthmatically:

"Alas! dear Mrs. Ruy-Bric, he was, indeed, deplorably Low!"

Not many philosophers strayed to Constance that season, yet now and then to some direct mind occurred a simple query, why could this couple do with impunity what was forbidden to youth and beauty? Why was their affair legitimate, when if pretty Jessie lingered a moment on the veranda, all the social harpies would descend upon her and tear her with their fierce claws? Why should making love with rosebuds be pernicious, and what saving grace was there in making love with pastry tarts! Why—but this *why* leads into infinite mazes. The difference 'twixt Tweedledum and Tweedledee must always obtain in worldly congeries, still it was a comfort to many to designate the constant intercourse of Mrs. Ruy-Bric and the Rev. Mr. Puggums as the ecclesiastical flirtation.

There were others who frequented the drawing-room, some of whom were and some were

not recognized by Mrs. High-Dudgeon. In the
hotel were also many families and individuals
that went their way and walked and drove and
boated, gayly unmindful of the social hierarchy.
But they were only foreigners. The English-
speaking element unanimously acknowledged
Mrs. High-Dudgeon.

The High-Dudgeon and all her subjects were
now breathlessly awaiting the advent of Miss
Vanderpool in their midst. Tony let them
wait. Every day the fabulous tales of the Vanderpool fortune, family, and power grew in
magnitude.

"They may be a trifle exaggerated, dear Mrs.
High-Dudgeon," Mrs. Ruy-Bric said one day.
"One must make allowances. Still, where there
is smoke there is always fire. The general impression seems to be that her fortune is limitless.
Happily she also has family. Great wealth
alone is so vulgar. There can be no doubt, she
is somebody."

"She is a lady!" replied Mrs. High-Dudgeon,
glaring about the room as if seeking the luck-
less wight who should dare to contradict her.

"And, oh, dear Mr. Puggums, if the sweet
creature would but interest herself in our enter-
prise!"

"And, oh, dear Mrs. Ruy-Bric, what a privilege that would be for her!" responded Mr. Puggums ecstatically.

"She was not at the service yesterday," the lady said, shaking her head mournfully.

"She may have been ill, let us always bear in mind."

"You are so charitable, so magnanimous, dear Mr. Puggums!"

"It is but my duty," he replied, stroking himself.

"Miss Vanderpool is so sweet-looking, so interesting."

"She is spiritual," wheezed little Mr. Puggums. "She should be one of us."

CHAPTER IV.

MISS AURELIA IS LAUNCHED AND BECOMES A SOCIAL SUCCESS.

When, one evening, Miss Aurelia drifted into the archipelago, all the little isolated feminine groups stopped talking and looked at her. This was not reassuring. She had gained considerable self-possession during the previous few weeks, but this ordeal was too much for her newly-fledged powers, and in a great tremor she dropped upon the nearest chair. She was therefore innocently grateful when Mr. Puggums toddled over the shining floor from that sacred spot where Mrs. High-Dudgeon sat enthroned amid her worshippers, and when he, with his most unctuous smile, begged the stranger to join that august group.

Miss Aurelia blushed, smiled, fluttered, and accepted his invitation. As she walked across the room, looking very tall and slight beside the globular Mr. Puggums, every eye was fixed upon her. Thanks to Tony, she presented a

most creditable appearance. The careful and decided arrangement of her hair lent character to
the shape of her head. Soft and judicious
puffs concealed the lankness of her figure. The
cut of her black grenadine was faultless, and a
nameless something betrayed the thorough lady-
like toilet, equally removed from pretence and
negligence. Yet every woman in the room gave
an unconscious sigh of relief, and the fiat of ap-
proval went forth. "Not precisely beautiful,
you know, but so interesting, so feminine,"
murmured one person of social weight. "Distinguished," said another. "Graceful, don't you
think so?" whispered a third.

In short, no one said anything unpleasant.
Benevolence and charity predominated. The
secret of this unusual reception of a strange
woman by her own sex lay, it must be confessed, in Miss Aurelia's personality, which pro-
voked no envy, hatred, or malice. So decided-
ly the reverse of provocative was it, indeed, that
her sisters, as they surveyed her charms, unanimously concluded to permit her to enjoy wealth,
social prestige, and a good character, and felt
that there were certain compensations in life
for people of smaller incomes and less conven-
tional renown.

Let us admit that there are women — not, of course, your kind of woman or my kind of woman—who strenuously oppose the unequal distribution of the gifts of the gods. They grant that a woman is pretty, if they can add, "Poor dear, it's a pity she's so stupid," or they admit that she is clever, provided they can say, "But how unfortunately plain." If, however, a woman's beauty and brightness are too palpable for even them to deny, they are sure to find something very serious the matter with her moral character. To concede that one and the same woman is beautiful and clever, good, warm-hearted, rich, and socially important—no, they would die first! Nothing, then, in Miss Aurelia's appearance or demeanor clashed with these firm and widely-diffused principles. It is, indeed, touching to observe what boundless trust freckles, sandy hair, and a wide mouth are apt to inspire in the average feminine heart.

Mrs. High-Dudgeon, with some effort, raised one of her dangling, purple satin arms and extended a puffy hand of welcome. No other mortal had ever been received with this distinguished mark of favor, and a flutter of surprise was perceptible in the room. Miss Aurelia thought that they were all very kind and civil,

though a little queer. Perhaps that was because she was unaccustomed to the English, who
were, she had heard, often eccentric. Partly
through the influence of their encouraging
smiles, partly from her nascent self-respect, she
was more at ease than she usually felt with
strangers, and Uncle John would have been vastly surprised had he seen his hitherto shrinking
niece the centre of an admiring group, the cyno-
sure of all eyes, unblushing, unapologetic, almost unconcerned. But it is only fair to add
that Miss Aurelia had not the remotest suspicion of her own greatness; moreover, whatever
may have been her human frailties, she was emphatically not a snob.

She said little, which was fortunate, as the
others, with the exception of the being in royal
purple, said a great deal. But Miss Aurelia
could not open her lips without receiving the
flattering tribute of profound attention, followed
by ejaculations of interest, pleasure, and admiration. She happened to say that she found Constance very pretty, but, perhaps, less picturesque
than Lucerne.

"Miss Vanderpool thinks," began Mrs. Ruy-
Bric, to her next neighbor, repeating the remark
with as weighty a mien as if she were communi-

cating an aphorism of Hippocrates. "Miss Vanderpool thinks," echoed another, until the innocent observation was conveyed to the outskirts of the High-Dudgeon coterie, where somebody was amiable enough to rise and convey the precious utterance to the next bevy of women, who, if not quite High-Dudgeonites, were still very select indeed, and careful to look down upon their neighbors on the other side. Like a ripple on the surface of the water, the valuable information spread over the whole archipelago, until from the most remote corner a voice was heard announcing with enthusiasm, "Miss Vanderpool thinks."

Miss Aurelia was at first somewhat bewildered. Her pale cheeks flushed slightly, her quiet heart beat faster than was its wont. But she breathed in the strong fumes of this incense with grateful nostrils, and began to consciously choose her words.

An enchantingly pretty American girl of seventeen, whose mamma was a candidate for the outer chair of the next to the High-Dudgeon group, had the temerity to peep in "to get a glimpse of the phenomenon," she said. She was, for various reasons, not in favor at court, and the ambitious mamma, fearing the downfall of

her schemes, reproved her daughter for so much
as showing her saucy head within the precincts.

"Well, mamma, it warn't worth while. She's
homely enough, I must say."

"Jessie, how often have I told you to say
ugly. Homely, in that sense, isn't English."

"Neither am I, thank goodness, and neither's
Bob. (Bob was her brother, a very bad little
boy, who was always going fishing, and falling
off the bridge, or tearing his trousers, or doing
something or other of a disreputable character.)
But, mamma, why do they make such a fuss
over her? She's mild as a lamb, but not a bit
smart, I guess."

"Clever," corrected the much-tried mother,
"and 'think,' not 'guess.'"

"Well, clever, then. Anyhow, she's a regular
stick. How do you say that in English?"

But hers was merely the voice of ingenuous
youth, and, as usual, it was lost in worldly fogs
and distances. Within the drawing-room the
sentiment was unanimous. Miss Aurelia pleased
and was pleased. They initiated her into the
tortuous mazes of the feud, and the follies of
the Inselites. They destroyed the characters of
all the hotel guests, outside their charmed circle.
And they persistently invited her contempla-

tion of a church at that time building in a vil-
lage with an unprononnceable name in Wales.
She found the tales of the Inselites very amusing; laughed gently over the idiosyncrasies of
her neighbors, but, while she listened politely,
she wondered that they should take such pains
to describe the prospective decorations of a
structure which she, in all probability, would
never have the pleasure of seeing.

"I should think it might be very pretty," she
replied, civilly.

"Oh, do you? I'm so glad, Mr. Puggums,
Miss Vanderpool thinks it might be very
pretty."

"All we need is a few devoted and pure
spirits," he gurgled. "I felt sure that you, my
dear young friend, would take an interest in it.
I am gratified and encouraged."

Miss Aurelia could not imagine why, and
merely looked at him seriously, which made
him hurriedly change the subject, fearing that
he had been more zealous than discreet.

She enjoyed her evening extremely. It was
to her, however, a novel kind of enjoyment and
somewhat fatiguing. Most women, half her age,
could swallow with ease as much adulation as
she was receiving. But this was simple-hearted

Miss Aurelia's first experience of the great world.

She began to long for seclusion, her wrapper, and blithe little Tony. Accordingly she rose, and bade her new friends good-evening, at an early hour, thanking them with great cordiality for their kindness. Now, no one of that party ever dared to make her adieux before Mrs. High-Dudgeon gave the signal. Miss Aurelia's independent action seemed, therefore, to accord with her reputed position, and created the best possible impression. "She is exclusive," they murmured, admiringly.

"She is a lady!" thundered Mrs. High-Dudgeon, as Mr. Puggums closed the door behind Miss Vanderpool's retreating form.

In the meantime Tony had not been idle. Having safely launched her bark upon a prosperous sea, wind and weather being all that the most sanguine soul could wish, she had descended to the lower regions to find out how the world wagged, knowing, what many philosophers ignore, that the world begins its gyrations down there.

And there in the servants' hall, where the groupings and prevailing views bore an extraordinary resemblance to those of the drawing-

room, she had heard something which made her
warm heart feel very sorry and pitiful. The
merry, big, blond man, whose office it was to receive the passengers of the Insel Hotel omnibus, in other words, the conductor, had made a
false step in climbing up to his place beside the
driver, and had fallen, and the great wheel had
passed over his leg, which was fractured in two
places and badly crushed. Some said it was
his fault, some said it was the coachman's fault,
and some shook their heads helplessly and wondered what his wife and his six children would
do when he was at the hospital, earning nothing.
Some regaled themselves with similar instances,
in which the crushed man died, the wife came
to an inexpressibly bad end, and the children,
as a matter of course, to the gallows.

Tony listened quietly, then skipped away.
Rapidly passing through various corridors and
rooms, she descended a private stairway and
penetrated unhesitatingly to the den of the
sphinx. In answer to her knock a gruff and
unintelligible sound seemed to accord permission to enter. The director in the visible
bureau above was accustomed to every kind of
apparition and complaint. The sphinx down
here counted his gains and matured his plans

undisturbed by mortal presence. Surprised, he stared grimly at her over his spectacles.

"Good-evening," she said, cheerfully. "Please give me a large sheet of paper for a subscription list for poor Thomas Straub."

He silently handed her a long blue sheet.

"Thanks. Now please give me another."

"What for?" inquired the eyes of the sphinx, who knew very well that one does not make money in this world by improvident gifts, even of paper.

"To make a rival subscription list to be circulated among the Insel Hotel people," Tony replied, demurely.

The serious-minded man smiled a strange smile, gave her a second long blue sheet, and took up his pen, but Tony did not go.

"Straub is very badly hurt, sir," she said, pityingly.

No response. The silent man turned down the gas slightly. For conversation one requires little light.

"He has so many little children, and they are so young. His wife is young, too, and half dead with grief and anxiety. And they are very poor."

Silence.

"He was such a fine, cheery man, sir, and has served you well many years."

Not a muscle of his face moved.

"They say he will be three months or more in the hospital."

Still silence.

"And so I wanted to ask you, sir," she continued, quite undismayed, "if the two hotels raise five or six hundred marks, if we can count upon you for another hundred or so. It would be kind and generous of you, sir."

No reply, but she knew that he was listening.

The fresh, bright voice went on with now and then a little quiver in it.

"How would you or I feel, sir, crushed and mangled and poor, and nobody to look after our families? Wouldn't we have more courage to bear the pain and get well, if we could know our fellow-creatures were sorry? Sorry with words—that's cheap business. Sorry with our pockets—that comes from the heart."

Again she waited, then began again:

"You are a rich man, sir. You are his employer. You not only can help him with your money, but you can do him more good than any one else in the world can, if he feels you are his friend in his misfortune. He looks up to you.

It will do his pride good, comfort him, comfort his heart and his leg, his soul and his body, if you stand by him now!"

Never before had a warm and womanly voice, in unselfish pleading, been heard within those four narrow, dingy walls.

"And—knowing my duty—if I may make so bold, you ought to stand by him. He was doing your work on small pay. It was your omnibus that crushed him, with its great, cruel wheel."

Now, curiously enough, the serious-minded man had a heart concealed somewhere in his organism, but no one ever took the trouble to reach it. From the nature of the situation, neither his heart nor the hearts of his summer guests were called conspicuously into action by their mutual relations. This small, clear-voiced, clear-headed woman had not reckoned in vain. Receiving, not giving, was his specialty; still, we all have latent talents.

He looked at her, and nodded slowly.

"Good," she said, turning to go. "I knew you would. I will come again. Two hundred marks I believe you said, sir?"

He smiled again at her cheerful tone of conviction, but nodded assent; then for the first time spoke.

Polly did look, but all she saw was her own face in the little
mirror of the fan which Tom held up.

"Who are you?" he asked.

"Tony, Miss Vanderpool's maid," she answered, with her pretty smile.

When Miss Aurelia ascended from the scene of her triumphs, Tony was waiting with a huge blue subscription paper in her hand. It was drawn up for the benefit of Thomas Straub, and was headed by Miss Vanderpool in large and masculine characters.

"I took the liberty to write the gracious fräulein's name to save her the trouble. I did not know for how much."

"But, Tony," remonstrated Miss Aurelia, aghast, "some rich person ought to head the list. I will give the poor man something so gladly; but it will be better for him if a rich person begins."

"I don't think that will make any difference," Tony replied, calmly.

Miss Aurelia did not wish to say more for fear of hurting Tony's feelings, but she continued to regard the paper with dismay.

"If the gracious fräulein would say how much she would like to subscribe."

"You see, Tony," began Miss Aurelia, with candid incoherence, "I have so much a month, and out of that I am in the habit of saving a

5

regular sum for private charities—old Mrs. John-
son and old Miss Beale—but, dear me, I forget,
you don't know them, and my accounts are very
confusing to me, although I certainly give them
great attention, and when they won't balance
Uncle John helps me out; and so, with the new
grenadine, I don't exactly know where I am."

"The gracious fräulein has no need of balancing accounts," replied Tony, encouragingly.
"If a girl like me couldn't," shaking her head,
gravely, "that would be very bad. But it is so
arranged that we always can," she added, modestly. "Could the gracious fräulein spare twenty marks?"

"Oh, Tony! of course. But what is five dol-
lars to head a subscription? I can give ten;
but—"

"Ten? That is forty marks. Now we are
safe. We shall have a small fortune for Straub.
If the gracious fräulein allows I will quickly put
down 40 opposite her name, and take the paper
to the drawing-room while the ladies are still
there."

"But, Tony—"

"It is quite right. It is perfect." Off flew
Tony with the paper.

She returned an hour later, with a long list,

and success beyond her fondest expectations.
Five hundred marks were promised her for
Straub. The other blue document, under the
control of a trustworthy waiter, was already in
circulation at the Insel, with the statement of
the sum raised at the Constanzer. "If charity
won't spur them on, competition will," thought
Tony. "I don't care why they give as long as
Straub gets the money."

This reflection she did not confide to Miss
Aurelia, nor did she relate the interesting de-
tails of her tour round the hotel. How she
composedly entered the drawing-room and smilingly presented the paper to no less a personage
than Mrs. High-Dudgeon. How that lady had
made a wry face, but put her name down for
fifty marks, reasoning that she could not allow
even Miss Vanderpool to seem to prescribe to
her the extent of her benevolence, and, as lead-
er of society in Constance, she should be reluctant to give less than an unmarried woman.
She comforted herself with the thought that, to
the best of her knowledge, no man in Constance
had ever before made himself an object of charity by getting under the wheels of a hotel omnibus, and she trusted anything so inconvenient
might never again happen. The general would

simply have to wear his old dressing-gown three
months longer.

Mrs. Ruy-Bric gave forty marks. She smiled
gallantly, but her soul writhed. "Painful as it
is, I must hold my own with her for the sake
of the little church in Wales," she murmured
to Mr. Puggums, who gave—his blessing.

Some one indiscreetly expressed surprise that
Miss Vanderpool had not contributed more.
"But you know people of immense wealth are
always parsimonious," replied another. Tony,
not understanding the words, but keenly alive
to the language of intonation and mien, found
occasion to introduce a somewhat ornate version
of what Miss Aurelia had just mentioned in regard to her private charities. This interesting
item was added to the floating bits of gossip
about Miss Vanderpool.

Introduced under such auspices—Miss Vanderpool's charity—the subscription naturally proved
a success. It became the fashion, the enthusiasm of the moment. Up and down the long
drawing-room went modest-looking, smiling little Tony, with her long blue paper and her deferential, pretty ways. "Miss Vanderpool's own
maid," they whispered. Everybody gave; many
from pure kindness of heart, some because oth-

ers gave. Jessie's mamma made a fatal mistake. She happened to be the only person in the house with genuine silver-mine connections; but, having no ambassador to properly present her before the foundations of society, her claims to public veneration were unknown. Thinking to please or impress her neighbors, she signed her name with a flourish, and, taking out her purse, gave Tony a hundred-mark bank-note on the spot. From that evening Mrs. High-Dudgeon did not recognize her. It was the deathblow to her social aspirations. Still, Thomas Straub's wife and children lived several weeks on the twenty-five-dollar donation which vanity had prompted.

Miss Vanderpool's name carried everything before it. Then Tony had a wonderfully keen eye. Where a face showed one benevolent yielding line, there she stood with her blue paper and her magnetism.

The Insel Hotel guests, as she had anticipated, also gave liberally. Determined not to be outdone by the Constanzer, and aggrieved that the latter had taken the initiative in a matter which, after all, concerned their own omnibus, they indignantly contributed six hundred marks to the support of the unfortunate man's family.

Tony took the two subscription lists and the cash down to the serious man in his den. He read the names, counted the money, and added his promised two hundred marks, after which they performed the ceremony of shaking hands heartily. She deposited the money in the bank, and joyfully carried the receipt for it, and the subscription papers, to Thomas Straub's young wife. On the Constanzer list " A. Z." was written very small indeed; and who could suspect " A. Z." meant Tony. Opposite stood ten marks, which was a fourth of her month's wages. Straub's wife wept over her, and cried " Vergelt's Gott," and asked her whom she must thank. " I am only the maid," returned Tony, smiling with delight. " Thank Miss Vanderpool; she led the list."

CHAPTER V.

MISS AURELIA, having had greatness thrust upon her, gradually began to suffer from a complaint which in her lowly days she had never experienced—ennui. When shy and unknown, she used to steal into a hotel drawing-room, her book in her hand. She was at liberty to read if she wished, or to watch the people covertly, and indulge in innocent speculations about them. Occasionally some woman, also shy and alone, would speak to her. This had been pleasant, and made a little variety.

Her previous condition was, in short, freedom —the dove's conception of freedom, not the eagle's, but freedom all the same. Now she was in bondage. Every evening she took her appointed place. Every evening she heard the self-same phrases. Her own mental horizon was not vast, but, indeed, it stretched beyond the monotonous pretence and narrowness of ill-natured platitudes. She was not clever, but, at

least, she was clever enough not to call every
woman who happened to be cleverer or prettier
than she "second-rate." She began to weary of
it all, of the dull malice, of the habitual denigra-
tion, and especially of that ubiquitous little
church in Wales, which, wherever the conversation started, was always looming up in the
background with its pressing need of a thousand
pounds sterling to make it "so precious, so perfect, dearest Miss Vanderpool!" She wearied
of their voices, of their manners, and—oh, trea-
son—she even wearied of the purple satin and
all that therein was.

Afternoons it was not much better. Once
enrolled in those ranks there was no escape.
Frequently Mrs. High-Dudgeon's majestic and
dreary servant came with a few lines inviting
Miss Vanderpool to a social cup of tea at four
o'clock, "quite among ourselves." And there
they all were, six or eight satellites revolving
around the shining purple satin—Mrs. Ruy-Bric,
Mr. Puggums, and the little church in Wales.

Even mornings she had no peace, for dearest
Miss Vanderpool was affectionately solicited to
bring her embroidery over to Mrs. Ruy-Bric's
balcony, where were also the Rev. Mr. Puggums
and the L. C. in W.

For these rites Tony zealously dressed her mistress, and congratulated herself that Miss Aurelia was enjoying life at last. Tony herself would have found no entertainment in such staid diversions. A glass of beer at a little table in a shady garden with somebody who knew her well and loved her; cheerful couples at other tables, a swarm of children in their Sunday pinafores, everybody clean, kindly, and respectable, and a band playing away like mad—this was nearer Tony's idea of enjoyment. But she knew English-speaking people liked to take their pleasure lugubriously, and was liberal enough to be willing that they should be happy in their own way. She knew that in a Continental hotel frequented by the English, and boasting a permanent set of English lodgers, there must always be a perpetual ferment and striving for social recognition, and that lakes and mountains have no power to calm and satisfy the soul, if the leading lady does not receive one; it was also her firm conviction that most English-speaking people are wretched if not noticed by somebody quite inferior to themselves.

Already Miss Aurelia looked like a different being, wore faultless toilets, carried herself with considerable self-possession, was the pride of the house, had become, indeed, so celebrated that the Insel Hotel had set up an heiress of its own, to compete with her. Tony was satisfied with her work. But Miss Aurelia — alas! she was not happy.

Why, she did not know. Everybody was so attentive, she reproached herself for her ingratitude. She had singular thoughts about Mrs. High-Dudgeon and the others, and she feared she had become very wicked indeed. If she could only have seen herself and them and laughed! But she took them all seriously, and grew daily more confused. Church and Sunday caused her many misgivings.

At home she had been considered fairly religious, as she always went to church Sunday mornings if it did not rain; and at the Lenten services, when the clergyman said "Dearly beloved brethren," she was usually one of the intrepid band of women in the cold vestry whom he addressed under this flattering title. She could not remember that in church at home she had ever had unholy thoughts. But in the room appropriated by the English for their Sunday services she was conscious of irregular impressions from which her conscience recoiled. In the first place, try as hard as she would, she could

not make it seem like church, with the click of
the billiard-balls in the next room but one, and
children shouting French on the lawn, and a
splendid chorus of men's voices singing German
love-songs in a beer-garden a short distance beyond the hotel. In the front row of worshippers stood Mrs. Ruy-Bric in a Paris toilet, making
profound courtesies to the deity. Mr. Puggums
preached upon the necessity of supporting English chaplains in Continental hotels; plainly inti-
mated that he was living upon the voluntary contributions of the little congregation, which he
reproached with asperity for its shortcomings in
this respect. Was it quite delicate to speak so,
Miss Aurelia timorously asked herself. Was
Mr. Puggums's support an imperative condition
of the spiritual growth of those present?
Couldn't people read their prayer-books in their
rooms? Or, if they chose to gather together,
could they not be less conspicuous, less aggres-
sive? Need they take possession of one of the
public reading-rooms? What if the Lutherans,
or the Roman Catholics, or the Spiritualists
should proceed in this masterful manner? Why
the English, in view of so unpardonable a liberty, would leave in a body. The foreigners bore
it amiably enough. They shrugged their shoul-

ders and said, "They are English; what can you expect?" Still, should not one consider other people's rights even in the exercise of one's religion?

Near her, two bright-faced boys sat uneasily on the hard dining-room chairs which the grinning waiters had brought in and arranged under Mr. Puggums's fussy directions. The boys, when they dared, looked longingly out of the window towards the lake, shining and warm under the August sun, and gleaming temptingly through the trees. And if they were on the water, in the water, what then? Would it not profit them at least as much as to be scolded by Mr. Puggums because the contributions were not lavish? "Oh, how wicked I am!" she thought, and spasmodically listened to Mr. Puggums's discourse; but the sounds from without attracted her, and again her mind wandered. There was, after all, something amiable about the ungodly, something gentle and winning. She had often, especially in these latter days, noticed a family of Portuguese, she imagined, at all events, they were very, very foreign. There were seven children, with sweet voices and dusky, loving eyes, and the oldish father and mother sat often on a garden bench, actually hand in hand. They had a title or two in their own land, which they used simply as a matter of course—not being accustomed to anything better—and they entertained old-fashioned ideas about courtesy and loyalty. Three of their little girls were pushing the ivory balls about, counting five when they pocketed one, and some of their boys were playing with the great Leonberger dog on the lawn. None of them were making much noise, and their pretty voices sounded glad and innocent. Miss Aurelia sighed to think that the path of virtue could be so thorny.

This memorable Sunday was oppressively warm. Extreme heat and cold, according to criminal statistics, produce desperation in the human mind, and the temperature may have been in part responsible for Miss Aurelia's abnormal condition. She never before was pursued by such thoughts, never was so sadly conscious of depravity. At dinner, even the much-thumbed and tattered rubber plants which adorned the *table d'hôte* were curling up in utter recklessness; the waiters skimmed about with an exhausted air, and the frescoes of natural and historical scenes along the lake of Constance—landscapes at which the guests were apt to stare between the courses—seemed to pro-

ject rays of tropical heat from their glaring sur-
faces.

Opposite Miss Aurelia, Mrs. Ruy-Bric surrep-
titiously loaded Mr. Puggums's plate with sweet-
meats. Neither his appetite nor her devotion
were affected by the outward caloric. Near her
Mrs. High-Dudgeon looked most portentous and
forbidding. Across the room, at a separate table, sat the ungodly Portuguese family, after all
their Sabbath-breaking, cool, comfortable, and
unconscious of their sins. The dark-eyed girls
were dressed in simple white, the father smiled
at his eldest boy, the mother was as motherly,
affectionate, and contented as mortal woman
could be. Miss Aurelia contemplated them, and
her wicked thoughts continued.

That afternoon she again attended divine service in the reading-room, and felt singularly
unhappy and depressed. Afterwards Mrs. Ruy-
Bric whispered to her that they all depended
upon their sweet Miss Vanderpool to join them
in the drawing-room that evening, where they
should sing psalms and hymns. It was really
a duty where there was so much levity; otherwise people would amuse themselves. Miss
Aurelia shuddered.

She went up to her room, where Tony was
arranging the jalousies and singing blithely.

"What have you done to-day, Tony? Have you enjoyed yourself?"

"And how much!" exclaimed the girl. "First I went to mass, and then I arranged everything for the gracious fräulein, knowing my duty, and this afternoon, with gracious permission to go out, I enjoyed myself vastly. The garden was breezy and cool, the people so kind, the music beautiful. Then the sail over and back! The gracious fräulein knows I am a miserable coward in a small boat. But a big steamer with music and an awning. Ah!"

Miss Aurelia looked at her long and wistfully.

"Tony," she began, after a pause, "do you not know some nice place where we could go, and where"—she hesitated, coughed, gasped, blushed, looked frightened, knew that she was wicked, yet was impelled to go on—"where there are no—no English?"

Tony turned quickly and scrutinized her mistress.

"Why yes, surely," she replied, smiling.

"I mean where there are foreigners."

"And you a New England woman!" moaned her conscience.

"Oh, yes, I know places where there are nice

Germans and French people, so amiable, and of excellent family."

"I don't think I care about much family," said Miss Aurelia, plaintively.

"Oh, it's a very different thing," returned Tony, in quick response to Miss Aurelia's thought. "I know a place where there are counts and barons and now and then a prince or two, but they are easy about it and kind to all the world, like those distinguished Portuguese."

"That's what I mean," said Miss Aurelia, brightening, "kind people."

"Now and then an English-speaking person may happen along," Tony reflected.

"Oh, I shouldn't mind that," Miss Aurelia returned, magnanimously, "that is, if she didn't stay too long, and was not too—too—

"Proper!" suggested Tony, demurely.

"Or too severe," Miss Aurelia ventured to add.

"And dull," said Tony.

"And puffed up."

"And domineering."

"And censorious."

"And solemn as an owl."

"And if she would not always call her neighbors second-rate."

"Or sing out of tune."

"Or talk about High Church decorations, or diseases; but, oh, Tony, I fear we are very wicked."

"Not at all, not at all!" she declared, with a jolly little laugh.

"You see, Tony, I am so tired of some things, and I have such a longing to be among people who are kind and who enjoy themselves."

"Of course. And what is more natural and right? Ought the gracious fräulein to wish to be among people who are unkind and do not enjoy themselves or let anybody else enjoy anything?"

"Well, Tony, you may pack. We will leave to-morrow."

"Very good, gracious fränlein."

"And, Tony, I think I would like to take a stroll along the lake. Do you happen to know any little way out, that would not lead past the drawing-room or the broad piazza, or anywhere in fact where I might meet—might meet—"

Presently Miss Aurelia was sauntering down a secluded garden path, while Tony rapidly and systematically began the work of packing.

"I have made a mistake," she admitted.

6

"She doesn't like it. It is too heavy for her,
and no wonder. Never mind. It has improved her. She will enjoy herself all the
better next time, and she's a dear, good, innocent, sweet - tempered lady. When we get
among the real ones she'll be contented as a
kitten."

Meanwhile Miss Aurelia wandered on, her
thoughts in a strange whirl. She was elated
by the prospect of escape, and proud of her
unwonted energy and initiative.

On a garden bench sat the oldish Portuguese
couple hand in hand, quiet, contented, gazing
silently at the lake. "That is pretty — very
pretty," thought Miss Aurelia as she passed, a
strange sensation, neither very sad nor yet
pleasurable, and which she chose to call "a
little homesick," taking possession of her. She
was far too proper to consciously wish somebody would sit by her and hold her hand in
the twilight, but she vaguely suspected that she
had not got as much out of life as some people.

Suddenly she met a young gardener, with his
wife and child, coming home from their Sunday outing. The little thing was tired and
fretful, and the father swung him up to his
own strong shoulder, while the mother com-

forted him with the loving tone that makes
any voice and any language sweet. "How
happy everybody is!" sighed Miss Aurelia.
She was herself by no means unhappy. On
the contrary. For she remembered the forbidding circle assembled in the drawing-room
and waiting in vain for her. She should, perhaps, never see them again! She and Tony
would slip away by the first train, before any
one was aware of their intentions. Delightful
thought.

She stood on the shore. The lake lay before
her with long golden gleams reflected in its
placid depths. The sky was beautiful with the
last lingering glories of the sunset. The old
monastery held itself bravely above the tree-
tops. Beneath the arched bridge, with its ancient statues of warriors and dignitaries, the
strong Rhine stream swept on in haste.

In her unwonted warm and receptive mood
Miss Aurelia's thoughts assumed defined shapes.
The reaction from the High-Dudgeon and Ruy-
Bric influence drove her into untrodden paths
of reflection.

"Yes, I should really like to be among people who are kind and who enjoy themselves
exactly as they please, without knowing that

they are doing wrong." This may be incoherent, but it is precisely what Miss Aurelia was thinking. Then she grew a little troubled, for the problems which circumstances and her mental development had created were surely rather perplexing.

"Is being kind, being good?" she asked herself, searchingly. " It almost seems so to me, although I fear I am very wicked to even think of such a thing. I must talk about it all with Mr. Brown when I return home, and tell him about the billiard‑balls pushed about by those gentle little girls. I think it is pleasant when people don't know that they are doing wrong. It is certainly pleasanter than when people are so dreadfully sure that they alone always do right. At all events, since I am over here, simply travelling for pleasure, I would rather see the happy people. And it seems to me, if we don't like what foreigners do, and if we consider them so bad, we'd better stay at home. Of course there are things that they do Sundays which we couldn't possibly do. Beer and music, under a tree, for instance. I don't know that the beer is wrong, or the music, or the tree; but the combination does seem wicked. That is, for me. But is it for Tony? Mr. Brown, himself, told me once he did not think a quiet drive in the woods Sunday afternoon in itself a sin. Then, so far as beer is concerned, most people at home have their best dinners Sunday. Dear, dear, it is very confusing. And if a phaeton in the woods is not a sin, why is a boat on the water?

"I do want to see foreigners and happy people—families and children. And I would like to see more men. Not, of course, for myself," she assured herself with a maidenly blush, "but I do like to see them about, that is when they are not as short and fat as Mr. Puggums, or so infirm as poor old General High-Dudgeon. I'm afraid he isn't very happy! It does seem natural and cheerful to see men with their families. The Portuguese gentleman, for instance—and the gardener, just now, was very nice."

Miss Aurelia's innocent cogitations were founded upon fact. Cleopatra would have had a sad time of it at the Constanzer Hof, for there were "no men to govern" there. Or, to be quite accurate, there were a few feeble representatives of the stronger sex, but they were already so thoroughly governed that Cleopatra herself could not have won a single glance from their weary, sad, and downcast eyes. Miss

Aurelia considered them categorically, and found herself dwelling with a kind of guilty pleasure upon the conspicuous exception to them all, the lord and master of the handsome, smiling, immoral, happy Portuguese family.

"I must really talk with Mr. Brown. I hope he will not find too great laxity in my views. I have often heard that European travel unsettles one. Yes, I must certainly talk with Mr. Brown."

She was now walking along the shore road directly by the water. There were pleasant seats under the trees, and the air was soft and still. Boats were gliding about far and near. She listened to the rhythmical dip of the oars, and to songs from gardens, voices and laughter. The identical melody, to which, in the Puggums church-service that morning, a hymn had been slowly and discordantly dragged along to the glory of God, now resounded at a rapid tempo, and sung with feeling and musical intonation by thirty trained voices, swinging and swaying passionately, in its original guise as an old German love-song.

"Why is it holy to sing it slow, and wicked to sing it fast?" she asked herself.

"It is really very confusing. Perhaps I'd

better go in," walking slowly on, reluctant to
leave the pretty scene, and conscious that she
had not courage to meet the hotel faction face
to face, and assert her independence.

"I will go as far as the steps and then turn."

They were broad marble steps, descending
into the lake, with a suggestion of Venice in
their stateliness and the water rippling always
against the stone.

She went as far as the steps but she did not
turn.

Leaning against the carved balustrade, in one
of the most graceful attitudes ever designed
by mortal man, stood a beautiful and picturesque youth. He was tall, slight, and handsomely sun-browned. He wore a jaunty blue-
flannel sailor-suit, coquettishly if not generously
open at the throat, and adorned with silver anchors everywhere that it was possible to apply
them. A critical eye might have found him,
to say the least, theatrical. Miss Aurelia gazed
at him entranced.

With an engaging smile, he pulled off his
cap. His teeth were as white, his eyes as blue,
as Tony's.

"Gracious fräulein," he said, "may I have
the honor of taking you out for a row?"

His well-cushioned little white boat bobbed temptingly up and down, and grazed the marble steps. He looked at her with bold, it almost seemed to her, with admiring eyes. No man had ever stood before her with that gallant air.

"You are—" she began, hesitatingly.

"Fritz Binder, at your service; boatman, fisherman, and guide. Acquainted with every fact of interest on the lake and particularly accustomed to ladies," he rattled off, with a fluency only attainable by means of infinite repetition.

Miss Aurelia looked at him innocently, wonderingly, rapturously.

"It is Sunday," moaned her long-suffering, highly-scandalized, New England conscience.

Fritz Binder sweetly smiled, pulled the prow of his skiff well up on the second marble step, and striding in with his long, athletic legs, deftly arranged the cushions in the stern. Holding the boat with one foot, the other placed firmly upon the step, balancing himself easily, he turned the whole battery of his dark blue eyes and winning smiles upon his victim.

She gave one backward glance towards the

"WITH AN ENGAGING SMILE HE PULLED OFF HIS CAP."

hotel where, in unimpeachable respectability,
the English circle was gathered about that little
church in Wales.   She looked cautiously up
and down the curving, dusky road.   From gardens and passing boats floated music and happy
laughter.   The lake was one vast expanse of
dim, rosy gold.

Motionless, silent, smiling, Fritz Binder
waited.

Call no woman discreet until she dies.

Miss Aurelia, with a long, fluttering sigh,
stepped into his little bobbing boat.

CHAPTER VI.

THE ROMANTIC BOATMAN FRITZ BINDER OVERTHROWS TONY'S BEST-LAID PLANS.

Tony the wise, it may be the almost too wise, virgin, with all her forethought, never suspected that while she blithely sang and whistled and folded and packed, the foolish virgin was reclining upon cushions and skimming over the golden lake. Entranced, Miss Aurelia watched handsome Fritz Binder's lazy, swaying motion, listened to the click of the oars in the rowlocks, the soft fall of the water drops from the blades, the thud of the waves on the prow. Against the fading sunset sky the towers of the old city and the arched bridge receded in mysterious dimness. The shores grew indistinct. On they sped in the warm, dusky, languid summer night.

Miss Aurelia, in plain English, let herself go. Tony had unwittingly set powerful machinery in motion. The repressed, timid, apologetic

being, once awakened and encouraged to self-
assertion, flattered and strengthened in her
opinions, was taking unconscionable leaps
along the path of personal liberty.

She was perfectly aware that she was doing
something extraordinary and reprehensible.
"Some day you will repent of this sorely,"
protested the stifled voice of conscience from
the hidden recesses of her nature, where she had
relentlessly thrust it. "Let that day take care
of itself," replied her new-born recklessness.
Other boats glided past them. Other people
were enjoying themselves, she thought, accus-
toming herself to her wickedness. The stars
came out and the town lights. There was music from gardens and rowboats and sailboats.
The lake seemed vast and dark, yet furrowed
under the stars by happy little skiffs full of
melody and laughter. "I am wicked, you are
wicked, they are wicked," reflected Miss Aurelia,
not with poignant self-reproach, but merely in
a matter-of-course way, admitting the fact as she
leaned back comfortably against the cushions.

Meanwhile handsome Fritz Binder had not
spoken. He was content with the silent elo-
quence of his costume, his attitudes, and his
personality. He had rowed too many years on

the Lake of Constance not to know something
of the feminine heart. Princesses and peasants,
widows, spinsters, and school-girls had fallen
victims to his charms. Why, indeed, should
he seek to hasten the inevitable development
of things?

Lazily lying back on his oars, at length he
said, in a gentle, musical voice,

"The gracious fräulein has not been here
long?"

"Three weeks."

"Ah, I forget," he returned, with graceful
nonchalance. "I myself have been absent.
The Prince Botowski positively insisted upon
my accompanying him on an extended tour
round the lake. I could not refuse, although it
was rather a bore. He would not take no for
an answer, and we are like brothers, the prince
and I. Otherwise I should at once have remarked the gracious fräulein. Anything distinguished and elegant among the summer
guests I always remark. I have a great deal of
experience."

Miss Aurelia curled herself still closer
against the cushions, and felt singularly comfortable and happy. The stars grew brighter.
She glanced over her shoulder at the city. It

was a low, irregular mass far behind them, a
row of lights marking the shore.

They passed a villa, dark except for a dim
light in an upper room.

"That is the abode of a monster," said Fritz
Binder.

"Oh!" exclaimed Miss Aurelia, straining her
eyes to see it.

"A monster," he repeated, emphatically.
"A man who hates women and flowers is nothing less. He employs only men servants. He
has had all the roses in his garden pulled up by
the roots, and flung over the wall. I would
not allow him to put his foot in my boat for
love or money. Money, he's got enough of.
But love, he knows nothing about. Not he,
the wretch!"

"You speak with feeling," stammered Miss
Aurelia.

"I do," returned the young man, in a still
more impassioned tone. "A man who despises
roses and flings women over his wall."

Miss Aurelia laughed.

He knew that she would laugh. He paused,
indeed, to give her the opportunity.

The romantic boatman laughed too—apolo-
getically.

"I beg pardon," he said. "But how can a man choose his words when he is boiling with indignation—and I, who love flowers and adore women!"

Miss Aurelia hardly knew what to reply or whether to reply at all. She was fairly blushing in the darkness, and felt that this conversation was becoming extremely intimate. But what an extraordinary young man! What refinement, what depth of sentiment.

"There," he remarked, in a less amorous tone, as they passed another villa, "lives Count Eyglas with his three beautiful daughters. The youngest, Countess Olga, is the image of yourself. A lovely creature of twenty-two. When the gracious fräulein came along towards the steps, I thought she was Countess Olga."

Whatever Miss Aurelia ought to have felt at this moment, the truth is that she was in no respect offended at being likened to a beautiful young countess of twenty-two.

"She goes out rowing with you?" she asked, her voice somewhat excited and embarrassed.

"She?" laughed Binder, "of course. She and all fair ladies, far and near. Ah, gracious fräulein, women see that I adore them, that I am their slave. My heart is tender to a painful, to

an extraordinary degree. But what can I do?
It is my nature. It is my destiny. I suffer,
but I do not complain."

"Ah!" murmured Miss Aurelia.

"It is true," he sighed, rowing now with
the least possible effort, his voice tender and
melodious, "and I do not hesitate to say that I
am always in love. If I were not in love I
should die. I am in love now, deeply, desperately, and ah, how respectfully!"

What could he mean? Miss Aurelia shivered
with excitement.

"I am only a poor boatman," he remarked,
sadly. "I know my position but too well."

"Oh," said Miss Aurelia, touched and distressed, "as to that, I am sure a boatman can be
very nice indeed, and you know in America we
believe that there is no such thing as counts
and kings—I mean to say—"

"Some weeks ago," interrupted Fritz Binder, in a mournful manner, "there was a
teacher here from a school on the Rhine, with
nine young ladies. I rowed them about all
day. When they left there were tears in their
eyes. They were mostly from the nobility.
They gave me their photographs. And one of
them sent me this anchor [pointing to one of

the large ornaments dangling from his heavy
silver watchchain]. I have sixty-three anchors,
all given me by ladies; but what of that," he
exclaimed, vehemently, "if one was born for
better things?"

Miss Aurelia felt the deepest sympathy, but
hardly dared to intrude upon his private griefs
with the questions that trembled upon her lips.

"Enough!" he exclaimed, with a tragic gest-
ure; "it is the decree of fate."

Presently he began to hum a Strauss waltz
under his breath.

"He is concealing his sufferings beneath a
semblance of gayety," thought Miss Aurelia,
much agitated. "Poor, brave, unhappy young
man! how I wish I could help him! If I
should talk with Uncle John about him! If I
could but help him find his sphere."

Binder's waltz merged into a whistle, and he
rowed on a few strokes with commendable
cheerfulness for so great a sufferer.

Again his voice broke the silence and his
oars grew languid.

"In my letters I express myself. A letter I
once wrote always brings tears to my eyes.
'Dearest Amalie'—her name was Amalie—
'though parted by cruel fate, you are the bright

star that cheers my lone and barren path, and oh, Amalie, where'er your foot may stray, remember one true heart beats for you still, and is until death your faithful and ever desolate Fritz Binder.'"

"Did you write that? That sounds beautiful."

"Oh, yes, I wrote it," he answered, with considerable pride. There are more of them. I know them all by heart. "There was Sophie's. Perhaps you would like Sophie's better than Amalie's. 'Oh, Sophie, you are the sunshine that warms my lone and barren path, and though cruel fate parts our fond hearts, remember, so long as my life lasts, every breath I draw and every thought I think will be for you alone, my lost, but ever dear, Sophie, with true love from one who is faithful unto death, Fritz Binder.'"

"But did you love them both?" asked Miss Aurelia, timid and greatly confused. "Both Amalie and Sophie?"

"Them and more," rejoined Fritz Binder. "I never count, I always love. I am all love. I love now—madly, hopelessly, passionately."

"Oh, dear me! I am afraid it's getting late. Perhaps, you'd better row towards the hotel," Miss Aurelia ejaculated tremulously.

7

No, she was not mistaken. Her boatman drew a long and profound sigh. She, too, was agitated, but blissful.

"Shall I not repeat some poetry for you?" he asked, softly. "The young ladies from the school on the Rhine, mostly from the nobility, wept over my poetry."

"Oh, do," she murmured.

He began. The more he recited the less he rowed, in order not to break the effect of the metre, she concluded. It was the longest poem she had ever heard, and she could not sufficiently admire his memory.

The stanzas rolled forth from his lips with the regularity of machine-work. Miss Aurelia by no means understood it all, but the theme seemed to be very beautiful and touching. There were frequent allusions to forget-me-nots and weeping willows, and lovers shedding tears over each other's graves. Fritz Binder's magnetic cadences and the gathering darkness and the gentle rocking of the boat were very soothing. Like a baby in a cradle, Miss Aurelia fell asleep.

Lower, with the same lulling monotony, the boatman's voice continued, while his arms were all but motionless. It was a most remarkable poem. Various stanzas seemed to recur with curious frequency, and, after a while, the weeping willows and forget-me-nots and lovers' tears were mingled in inextricable confusion.

He must have repeated something like a hundred and seventeen stanzas, when he lighted a match and looked at his watch, his voice going on independently.

"Hm! so late!" he muttered, then yawned, and caused the boat to make a violent lurch.

Miss Aurelia started.

"That is a beautiful poem," she said, guiltily.

"It brings tears to every eye—to mine—as often as I repeat it," answered the soulful boatman.

She became suddenly aware that there was not another boat visible or audible.

"I really must go in," she said, alarmed.

"It is not so very late," he assured her. "I have often been out later with ladies." But he began to row fast towards the hotel. They were, indeed, not far away, for Binder had not over-exerted his muscles, but had limited his performances to a sheltered cove a few rods down the shore.

Presently the boat ran alongside the marble steps, where a bright gas-lamp was burning. He helped her out with lingering tenderness. Looking up at the picturesque, handsome youth, she felt embarrassed and tremulous. How could she offer such a being money.

"Seven marks, if you please," he said, in a business-like tone. "After nine o'clock it's night-tariff."

She slipped a ten-mark gold piece into his hand.

"I have no change," he observed, quickly.

"Never mind," she murmured.

A radiant smile played over the boatman's fine features.

"And at what time to-morrow shall I have the honor?"

"Ah, to-morrow," she returned, sadly. "To-morrow I am going away."

"It cannot be!" exclaimed Binder.

"I'm afraid so."

He made a desperate and dangerous movement.

"Unsay those cruel words, or I will throw myself into the lake!"

"Oh, please don't do anything rash," she begged.

"Then promise me this shall not be farewell. I might have known," he declared, gloomily, plunging his hand through his hair. "I am only a poor boatman. But"—throwing up his handsome head, gazing at the stars, and pounding his chest vigorously—"am I to blame that I have something here that beats?" he demanded, fiercely.

"No, you are not. Certainly not," replied Miss Aurelia, with emotion.

"Then stay," he implored.

"Why should I not, after all? What harm would there be? He is very, very romantic, but could anybody be more respectful? It would seem almost cruel to refuse." The quiet stars looked down upon the curious pair. The little waves plashed against the stone steps.

"Stay, oh, stay!" pleaded the sad and gentle voice. Again he leaned against the balustrade in his picturesqueness. The silver anchors shone resplendent in the gaslight. He held his cap in his hand.

"Well, I will; there!" ejaculated Miss Aurelia, laying her conscience prostrate.

Binder straightened himself.

"What time shall I come?" he said, quickly.

"At four."

"Very well," he answered, cheerfully. "Good-night, gracious fräulein. Sleep well."

" Good-night," turning away.

" The main garden-gate will be locked at this hour," he called after her. "In such cases they've always got in through the small gate at the left."

Such cases! What cases? They! Who? She experienced a vague discomfort. Was this exquisite, starlight, unique episode only one of many boating *tête-à-têtes ?*

But she was too excited to consider this point long, and hurried towards the hotel garden. As she opened the convenient little gate she paused, her heart fluttering wildly, and listened to the regular sweep of Binder's oars. He was whistling an opera air with scrupulous care in the execution of the trills.

"Heroic young man!" she murmured. "What marvellous self-control !"

The great hotel with its blaze of lights now loomed up before her, like a huge monument to conventionality, and reminded her of the full meaning of her social and moral transgression, yet nothing could quite destroy her exaltation of spirits. She approached the house slowly, dreading the moment of entrance. Suddenly, from a by-path, a little figure darted towards her. She saw that it was Tony, but there was scarcely time

to speak before the doors opened and they were
ushered obsequiously into the hotel corridor. The
light dazzled Miss Aurelia's eyes. Surely this was
another world from that tender, dusky, gliding
realm she had just left. Tony, with an important air, as if she had been several hours on
special escort-duty, a pile of wraps on her arm,
solemnly marched behind her pale and dazed
mistress. Only once did either speak, when
Tony, as she passed three or four staring waiters,
let fall, with admirable distinctness, a remark
about the rare beauty of Count Eyglas's rose-
garden. Miss Aurelia had no idea what she
meant, and scarcely heard, but Tony knew, and
the waiters heard, and with the positive accuracy which characterizes most of our remarks
about our neighbors, the whole hotel knew the
next day that Miss Vanderpool had passed Sunday evening in Count Eyglas's villa.

Once within the shelter of her own room
Miss Aurelia breathed more freely, but she
longed for solitude, and avoided meeting Tony's
conspicuously cheerful and unconscious glance.
Turning away quietly, she said:

"I do not need you to-night, Tony."

"Very good," assented the smiling little maid.

"And Tony"—Miss Aurelia's pale cheeks

flushed—"I have decided—I have concluded—
I have made up my mind—to remain a little
longer. You may unpack, Tony."

"Very good," returned the cheerful voice.

"Not to-night, of course," continued Miss
Aurelia, stammering, as she looked at the two
neatly and fully packed open trunks, "but to-
morrow morning."

"Very good, gracious fräulein."

Presently Miss Aurelia was left alone with
her delicious reveries.

Tony, in her little room across the corridor,
sat down with an air of absolute conviction,
nodding gravely.

"It's a man!" she said.

CHAPTER VII.

FRITZ BINDER TEACHES THE INFATUATED MISS AURELIA TO ROW, WHILE TONY NOURISHES SCHEMES OF VENGEANCE.

"A man"—reflected Tony; "that changes everything, that turns everything topsy-turvy. Well, it's a lesson to me. One ought always to be attentive even when one's packing for dear life. She was excited. She was pale as a ghost. Then she blushed. 'Tony,' she said, quite brisk and unlike herself—'Tony, you may unpack.' Her clothes and hair were damp. She's been on the lake with a man. The dear, good, innocent lady!"

The next day Miss Aurelia remained secluded in her room.

Mrs. Ruy-Bric sent her dear love, and they all had missed their sweet friend so very much, and could she be ill?

Mrs. High-Dudgeon invited her to four o'clock tea, "quite among ourselves."

Miss Aurelia returned best thanks to both ladies. She was not ill, but had a previous engagement.

She was astonished at her own fluency and boldness.

All day she waited nervously, fearing something would intervene to prevent her from realizing her dear hope. She was restless; could neither sew nor read; changed her dress repeatedly, and spent much time before her mirror when Tony was not there. A woman of a certain age, whom a handsome being of the other sex has likened to a lovely young countess of twenty-two, can hardly be expected to neglect her toilet. Miss Aurelia's costume to-day expressed fresh juvenility—a bright knot of ribbons at the throat, some blush roses on her hat —a general air of bloom and dewiness. Tony might have been blind for all that she seemed to observe of these preparations.

But when, towards four, Miss Aurelia stole softly out of her room, there stood Tony, conspicuously on duty, her hat on her head, on her arm wraps, on her face the repose of an unsuspicious spirit.

"But I don't need you," stammered the lady, dismayed.

"Oh, I can come perfectly, the sewing is so well along!" responded Tony.

Miss Aurelia stalked on moodily. What excuse could she give? Single ladies at the hotel, when walking and boating, were usually accompanied by their maids, if they had any. "Oh, dear, I wish I didn't have any maid!" she thought, all her clinging fondness for Tony in thankless abeyance.

A queer, vivid little smile flashed across Tony's face, and left it demure as before.

"The gracious fräulein is going for a walk in the woods, I presume?"

"No, I am not," said Miss Aurelia, curtly.

Down through the winding garden paths they passed, and along the shore road towards the marble steps, where the gallant Binder, in his unapproachable attitude, already stood. How Miss Aurelia's heart beat! With a rush of pride she could not refrain from looking to see what effect her hero was producing upon Tony. But that small person, having given the boatman one indifferent glance, was gazing searchingly up and down the shore, as if expecting the approach of some other individual. Seeing no one, extreme astonishment, for an unguarded instant, was revealed upon her quiet features.

Miss Aurelia was tremulously uncertain whether Binder did or did not squeeze her hand. But no, he could have done nothing so familiar. The fancied squeeze must have been produced by the legitimate necessity of steadying her as she stepped into the boat.

Tony who, unseen, had crossed herself, and commended her perishable body and immortal soul to all her saints, brusquely declined his assistance, and with a certain stoniness of aspect followed her mistress. Miss Aurelia thought she had never seen her look so unpleasant. " I never before realized how long and pinched her nose is," she reflected.

Tony's nose did look pinched, and her complexion became sallow, assuming various shades of green and yellow, with a suspicious whiteness about the mouth. She hated and feared a small boat as only an inland-bred German girl, of what may be denominated the upper-lower class, knows how to hate everything appertaining to that treacherous and hideous element, water. But not even the miserable feeling at the pit of her stomach could induce her to desert Miss Aurelia in this extremity. Tightly clutching the boat, she fastened her eyes steadily upon Fritz Binder's embroidered blue sailor-blouse,

far too much cut down at the throat for her
ideas of propriety, and with more loyalty than
logic, mentally ejaculated :

"And if I drown, I'll stay in this boat!"

Binder, putting off from the landing, rowed
well. People were standing there, admiring him
as a model of manly grace and strength, and he
was willing to grant them this joy. But no
sooner had he passed the bridges leading to the
bathing-houses, and the piers and seats where
idlers were lounging and fishing and reading,
than he palpably eased up, and presently he
struck into his favorite little cove, where the current pulled less forcibly, and where the row of
villas along the shore presented pleasing topics
of conversation.

Miss Aurelia watched him greedily. Yes, in
the strong sunlight he was as beautiful as yesterday in the gloaming. There was no doubt whatever about his personal appearance. His nut-
brown face was faultlessly oval, his mustache
drooped with silky chestnut ends, his bold blue
eyes roamed far and wide with a look before
which her shy gaze sank. "He is a perfect picture," she thought. "After all, it is well that Tony
came ; for if he should be tender and impassioned
now, I really don't know what I should do!"

Tony, meanwhile, had shut her eyes tight. During the starting of the boat, and its passage with what she considered appalling rapidity through fierce surges—the lake, in point of fact, was like glass—she suffered torments in rigid silence. Perceiving a decided slackening of the motion, she forced herself to open her eyes.

"Impertinent jackanapes, what a stare he's got!" was her immediate reflection.

"This is the house of a monster," began Binder's melodious voice.

Miss Aurelia smiled in anticipation of the chivalrous sentiments about to follow. She had heard them the day before, it is true, but in a certain palpitating frame of mind tender repetitions do not weary us.

The women and the roses were advantageously produced, likewise Binder's excessive tender-heartedness.

The boat was scarcely moving. Little Tony, clutching it tightly, hating it when it stirred, physically very uncomfortable, resolved to do her duty at any cost. Fritz Binder's like she had never seen. Quiet, watchful, her pale face as expressionless as she could render it, she made her observations.

She in turn puzzled him, but not long. For

he speedily ascribed her evident want of approbation to her dread of the water. "She'll get over that, and then she'll be like all the rest of them," he concluded, easily. "Nice, neat little thing; heaps more fun in her than in the long old one."

"She's afraid," he said aloud, with a good-humored laugh.

"She is unaccustomed to the water," Miss Aurelia began, eagerly. "But I—I adore it. Water, water! what is so beautiful as water? There's nothing so heavenly on earth as water!"

"Quite like Countess Olga, she, too, adores water. 'Fritz,' she often says—she calls me Fritz so sweetly—'Fritz, there's nothing in the world like water!'"

A jealous pang shot through Miss Aurelia's heart at the thought of another woman sweetly calling him Fritz.

"Beautiful creature, the Countess Olga," he continued, "quite in the style of the gracious fräulein. When I saw that graceful figure coming towards the steps, says I to myself, 'That's Countess Olga.'"

Miss Aurelia grew rosy with delight.

Antoninia Zschorcher pricked up her ears.

"Being obliged to go off with Botowski—a very good fellow the prince is, but would not take no for an answer— 'Binder,' said he, 'my dear Binder, I depend upon you.'"

"Ho, ho, that's the kind of a man you are!" decided Tony.

"And, off with him, I hadn't observed the new arrivals. Anything distinguished and elegant I always observe," with a tremendous stare at his happy victim.

His pleasant voice and smiling, comely face made sad havoc with her heart. He would row a couple of languid strokes, then rest generously, and gently speak. All that he said sounded this evening even more charming than the first time.

Presently Tony nerved herself to a species of heroism.

"Why do we always remain opposite the same house?" she demanded, although her misery was far less acute when the boat was quiescent.

"That's because you are not used to the water," he said, condescendingly. "It only seems so." Nevertheless he plied his oars with more vigor.

"It's awful," shuddered Tony, secretly. "But

if the gracious fräulein has come out for a row, she ought to have her money's worth. If staying on one spot is all that's required, she might as well sit in a boat on shore."

He soon diminished his muscular action and ushered in the boarding-school on the Rhine, and the nine young ladies—mostly from the nobility—who had bedewed his boat with their tears. Fixing his eyes upon Miss Aurelia, he repeated, nearly *verbatim*, his erotic peroration of the previous evening. She wondered, yet was subtly flattered, that Tony's presence did not deter him. On the contrary, he glanced easily from one to the other as he declared himself desperately in love at the moment, and his conviction that he should die if he were not always in that sensitive condition.

Tony gave a low groan.

"Do you feel ill?" Miss Aurelia asked, kindly. Finding Tony no impediment, she had recovered from her nervous irritability.

"Thanks," said Tony, "I am much better. I am beginning to enjoy it." She certainly looked better. On her cheeks was a slight flush such as might be produced by the sun or wind, or indignation, and her lips were compressed in a flexible mocking line.

8

Binder now alluded to mysterious hidden griefs. There seemed to be a certain irrelevance in his remarks. Miss Aurelia's imagination lavishly filled in the gaps.

"Dearest Amalie," he began, "though parted by cruel fate, you are the one bright star that cheers my lone and barren path; and oh, Amalie, remember wherever your foot may stray, one true heart—"

Tony at this point was seized with a fit of coughing so loud and convulsive that it would have damaged the effect of the most eloquent love-letter ever written; her face was concealed in her handkerchief, above which her very temples were crimson with mantling color. Miss Aurelia was sorry for her, but thought it a pity anything so touching as Binder's recitation should be interrupted.

"—beats for you still" he went on, imperturbably, as soon as her paroxysm had subsided, "and is until death your faithful and ever desolate Fritz Binder."

Tony continued to cough in a stifled manner behind her handkerchief.

"And Sophie," suggested Miss Aurelia sympathetically, longing to comfort him for all his lost loves.

Sophie's missive followed.

Suddenly he sprang up like a rampant lion.

"Tell me you are going to stay, that for a little while you will gladden my lone and barren path, or I jump!"

How ardent, how nobly reckless, he looked! Before Miss Aurelia, in her agitation, could find words to soothe him, a voice said, dryly,

"Well, you can swim, can't you?"

Binder sat down quickly.

"Tony!" exclaimed her mistress, in shocked reproof.

Binder was, however, not a whit disconcerted.

"Swim?" he replied, with his bright, young, boastful smile, "I'm the best swimmer on the Lake of Constance."

Miss Aurelia admired his rapid transitions.

"If you would be so kind as to repeat that beautiful poem," she pleaded, "that moved all those young ladies to tears, and I am sure it would have made me cry too," she added, zealously, "except that without the dictionary at hand the German construction is so difficult."

Binder began sonorously.

The poem was long, but by no means as long as it had been the night before. Tony nipped its growth in the bud.

" You've already said that about the willows,"
she interrupted, or caught him up sharply with :

"That's the fifth time Cunigunde has put
forget-me-nots in her hair."

"Yes, she liked them," Binder responded,
placidly.

"She's a sharp little thing. She is the kind
I like. After fooling about on the lake all day,
with such as the long one, it wouldn't be bad
to come home to a neat, quick-witted little
woman like her."

He looked long and smilingly at her.

She looked long and unsmilingly at him, then
reached over compassionately and put an extra
wrap over Miss Aurelia's shoulders.

" Thanks, Tony," said the lady ; " it is a little
fresh." It was such a relief that Tony really
did not interfere.

"I suffer," announced Fritz Binder, quite un-
expectedly. "I suffer incredibly. I have sixty-
three anchors, tokens of affection and remem-
brance from ladies. But, alas! the decree of
fate is immutable."

"You don't like to row?" inquired Miss
Aurelia, with timid sympathy.

He pulled off his blue cap and plunged his
hands through his thick brown hair.

"Never mind," he said, tragically. "A cold world spurns a heart like mine. Am I to blame that it beats?" frantically clutching his blouse.

"Oh, Tony!" murmured Miss Aurelia, extending her hand, appealingly.

"He'll get over it," answered the maid, with asperity. "Hadn't you better row a little by way of variety?" she demanded, too rapidly and with too much dialect to be intelligible to her mistress.

"Anything in the world to please you," returned Binder, fervently.

"What is it?" inquired Miss Aurelia, ill at ease.

"He is going to row now," Tony said, her voice odd and hard.

Miss Aurelia looked wonderingly at them, but her attention was engrossed by her boatman's magnificent strokes. "How strong he is, how masterly!" she said to herself, in triumph.

"You will stay?" he begged, with an enamoured glance.

"Well, I suppose there is no absolute necessity of my going quite yet," she replied, attempting to be arch.

"What time to-morrow?"

"At the same time as to-day," she murmured, with a lingering maidenly glance.

As she stepped out of the boat she was in no doubt whatever, on the contrary, knew that he gave her hand an undeniable squeeze; but—ah, the fatally easy *descensus Averni!*—already she regarded this little dereliction from the path of etiquette with indulgence.

"Shall you come, too?" inquired Binder, eagerly, as Tony, avoiding his touch, sprang from the boat.

She deigned no answer.

Miss Aurelia, fumbling with embarrassment in her purse, again presented Fritz Binder with a gold piece and required no change.

The two women; each absorbed in her own thoughts, walked up the garden paths.

Blithe as a canary-bird sounded the boatman's whistle as he rowed away.

"'A COLD WAVE SPURNS THIS HEART OF MINE.'"

CHAPTER VIII.

MISS AURELIA, TONY, AND FRITZ BINDER AT CROSS-PURPOSES.

MISS AURELIA sat in her low chair by the window and looked smilingly out towards the lake. It was too dark to discern anything beyond the nearest trees of the garden, but the picture in her memory was charmingly vivid. Even the jaunty ribbon-ends floating from Fritz Binder's sailor-cap she recalled with tender delight.

The peculiar softness of her reveries was no doubt due in part to their novelty. A vernal freshness characterized her sentiments. There is a prevalent impression that every unmarried woman has had her love-affair, her "opportunity," as maiden ladies delicately call a marriage offer. It being often unwise and always dangerous to oppose prevalent impressions, the question at large shall be here discreetly avoided ; and merely in the individual case of Miss Aurelia, and as a necessary fact in the study of her psychological problems, will it be stated that up to this epoch she had never had any love-affair or "opportunity" whatsoever.   Her sober wishes had never strayed farther than an eminently Platonic attachment to a gentleman who had lectured two winters in her native town, and, like all the ladies of the Rev. Mr. Brown's parish, she was wont to wreathe his sensible and slightly bald head with a more or less sentimental halo.   But nearer to the dangerous ground upon which, with a certain wistful curiosity, she had seen her friends marching off in couples her timid foot had never trod; and any attention more compromising than the offer of an umbrella, or a seat in a horse-car, or the opening of a door, she could attribute to no man living.

She had, indeed, gone so far as to think it must be very pleasant to be engaged to be married, though this, of course, was not a thing one could very well say.   She was apt to skip the descriptions and general conversations in novels that she might come quicker to the love passages—which in most romances begin to occur somewhere near the 278th page—and these she usually read three times at the first sitting. · Not that she liked silly books.   On the contrary, her reading was excellently well chosen, according to the monthly list suggested in a literary journal to which she was a subscriber. But she did like, now and then, a real love-story. Of late she had found more analysis than love in fiction, and consequently returned to her less modern friends, with whom the story is more important than philosophy. Miss Kavanagh's "Nathalie" was her favorite novel, and M. de Sainville her hero.

It would puzzle most people mightily to discover any resemblance between grave Monsieur de Sainville in his château and jolly Fritz Binder in his boat. Miss Aurelia found no difficulties in the comparison, in which all advantages were, it is needless to remark, conspicuously on the side of Binder. Pleasantly occupied in meditating upon their respective noses and voices, and what she called their souls, she was greatly disturbed by Tony, who, at this ill-judged moment, knocked and entered the room.

Unlike her usual direct and self-possessed manner, she stood still, in evident hesitation.

"Well, Tony, everything is in order, I believe," remarked the lady, eager to return to her absorbing employment.

"Gracious fräulein," began Tony, rapidly,

"the packing and unpacking is nothing at all. A lady has a right to change her mind, and it's my duty and my pleasure to change with her. But, gracious fräulein, there's something that I have on my conscience to say—knowing my duty."

Now, what one has on one's conscience to say is rarely palatable to the other party, and in this case Miss Aurelia could not fail to suspect that Tony was about to communicate something unpleasant about Fritz Binder. "No scandal shall influence me," she instantly resolved. "Poor, calumniated young man! Something tells me that he is truly noble. However misunderstood he may be, I am his friend."

Tony had every intention of finding out all available facts of Fritz Binder's career, and even a little calumny would not have been unwelcome to her; but she had had, as yet, no time for special detective service.

"What is it, Tony?" said the lady, coldly.

"It is this," returned the maid, deprecatingly; "and I wish there were any way to tell the gracious fräulein, without telling her, but there isn't. That Fritz Binder—I don't say he's a bad man; I don't know anything about him out of his boat, but in it he makes money—with his eyelashes. If he's said all that once, he's said it five hundred times. The love-making and his lone path—why, that's his stock in trade, like a carpenter's tools. Every lady has a right to her little pleasures—but—there, I've said it!"

"Tony," rejoined Miss Aurelia, deeply hurt, and wondering whether dignified silence or a warm defence of the aspersed being would be the more efficacious, "all I have to say is, I am perfectly astonished at you, perfectly. I thought you were such a very nice girl!"

Silent and distressed, Tony cast down her eyes. After a pause, she began, with much sweetness and modesty: "When I was working in Marseilles I often made mistakes in people before I knew the language easily. Half knowing a language is so dangerous. One can't judge. Of course the gracious fräulein has made great progress, still Binder is a foreigner and a man, and—"

"Which of us two would be likely to have the most discernment about my own individual affairs?" interrupted Miss Aurelia, with the air of an incensed mouse.

Tony gave her one half-pitying, half-pleading glance, then answered, meekly, "The gracious fräulein, of course."

"Well, then!" concluded the lady, in triumph.

"But—"

"Say no more, Tony."

This crisis passed, Miss Aurelia felt that she had evinced unswerving loyalty as well as judgment and tact. Tony's preposterous allegations made absolutely no impression upon her.

"Oh," groaned Tony, when alone, "oh, if it were only not a man! The very last day, and things in so good a condition, and she going on so nicely—through people's nonsense and hatefulness and all the ins and outs—and was so nice and quiet and everywhere looked up to; and now she's almost escaped me, because she's in love—the dear, good, innocent lady.

"Of course she wouldn't hear a word against him. Who would? Would I, myself, against Eduard? But then, to be sure, I've got a man worth having, and not an anchor-dangling lazybones, with a dreadful blue-flannel, low-necked shirt; and he ought to be ashamed of himself! And a woman may be a lamb when she's in her right mind, but when she's in love you can no more influence her against the object than you can coax a great fiery locomotive to take a quiet walk in the woods with you. Well, I've had a long rest since the countess, and my mistress is good as gold, with no harm in her heart for

anybody, and I'll take care of her—and we'll
see, Fritz Binder!"

Tony's troubles now began in earnest. To be
vigilant, yet to awaken no suspicion; to cheerfully accompany Miss Aurelia on the dreaded
aquatic excursions, and not let fear or nausea
dull her observation; above all, to sustain her
mistress's aristocratic prestige in the house, in
spite of her spasmodic mania for the water, and
her conspicuous avoidance of the mighty con-
clave—all this was by no means easy.

Fortunately for Tony, Miss Aurelia, at Binder's suggestion, chose, at this juncture, to take
lessons in rowing. She would have tried to
learn to fly had he proposed it. Every day she
was to be seen painfully and awkwardly pulling
against the current, blisters on her hands, but
joy in her heart. Tony was divided between
pity for her mistress and grim rage towards the
lazy, smiling boatman, who let himself be lux-
uriously rowed about, far and wide, scarcely
touching the oars. She secretly vowed personal vengeance when the time should be ripe. As
yet she had no distinct plans, and could only
watch and pray, growing each day more distressed and uncertain of the end as Miss Aurelia
grew more radiant.

Still, Tony could not deny that the rowing freak was a help, or what would be called, in law, an extenuating circumstance. It permitted her, for instance, to allude to the necessity of expanding Miss Vanderpool's chest. This theme, judiciously interlarded with the names of a couple of world-renowned doctors, was well started at the servants' table, and ascended with due rapidity.

All was grist that came to Tony's mill. "I will take care of her, whether I work above ground or under ground," she resolved. "Above ground I prefer; still, one can't always choose, and the world is so dull! Have they no eyes? Can they not see she has lost her senses? Why, the very statues on the bridge laugh when the poor lady goes under the arch, pulling for dear life against the stream, and so proud when that Fritz Binder, sitting there behind her ogling me, condescends to praise her. Can't they see she's got anchors everywhere, and a blouse like a schoolgirl, and a rolled-up sailor-hat, all to be more like him? Can't they see that I can't stop her, and nothing can stop her? Lord help us! If I speak she'll send me away, and then there'll be nobody to help her, and nobody to throw dust in people's eyes; and healthy dust it is for them, too! Why should they understand and laugh at her? Would that help matters? And yet—and yet—if she were anybody else, how they would jeer! How fortunate it is that she is very plain, and that I started her with a fortune!"

Yet, indulgent as Tony believed the world to be towards the eccentricities of the owner of unlimited millions and a plain countenance, she was daily in an agony of fear lest some one should set the ball rolling in the other direction, above all, lest some one should laugh. "Why they don't laugh is a mystery to me," she sighed. "If it wasn't my dear, good, innocent lady, I should laugh myself until I'd die. And no wonder that old Frenchwoman looked at her curiously the other day through an eyeglass, and called her '*une espèce d'Anglais!*'"

Miss Aurelia's face, unlike Fritz Binder's, did not brown handsomely under the August sun, but grew irregularly red, particularly on the end of her nose. It must also be confessed that she showed to less advantage in her piquant juvenile boating-costume than in the soft and sober draperies in which Tony's good taste had delighted to array her. Moreover, she was growing thinner each day, and her form was one that could ill bear a diminution of its charms.

Since she had begun to row the distances traversed were really considerable, for Binder manifested no want of energy in suggesting the longest possible tours. His combinations and fertility of resource were now most admirable, and nothing in the whole neighborhood was neglected. She rowed him to the Grand Duke's Schloss at Mainau, and was more than rewarded for her exertions when Binder bestirred himself sufficiently to pluck an ivy-leaf from the castle wall and present it to her. They made an excursion to Reichenau, and, listening to the romantic tale of Ekkehardt, Miss Aurelia cast enraptured glances at her graceful boatman, and only wished Ekkehardt stood there in the flesh beside him, that the world might see which was the greater hero. And when she paid her respects to the good parson who had invented Volapük—the world language—she longed, instead, for a tongue which she and Binder could alone command.

Tony begged to be allowed to learn to row, but this Miss Aurelia jealously refused. The little maid never grew sufficiently accustomed to the boat to feel quite comfortable or safe in it, but often she fancied that her continued, if slight, sensation of nausea might proceed as much from

acute disgust at Fritz Binder as from the motion
of the water. His manner to her, however, was
sensible and manly enough, and full of undis-
guised admiration. She did not dare, in Miss
Aurelia's presence, to be less than civil to him;
but she jumped in and out of the boat without
his assistance, avoiding his hand as if it were a
viper, and she scowled at him with appalling
fierceness whenever she could do so with impunity.

With all her pent-up resentment, she was wise
enough never, by word or look, to criticise him
before Miss Aurelia. It required her utmost
power of self-restraint; but after that first and
only rebuke she knew that she must be patient. One day she grew sick at heart, so great
were her impotent rage and displeasure. They
had had a long row. Binder had deigned to
accompany Miss Aurelia; that is, sitting behind, he had gently plied his oars in unison
with hers, meanwhile throwing tender glances
over her shoulder at Tony.

Miss Aurelia thought that it was heavenly.
It reminded her of the music of the spheres.
What harmony of soul! What rhythm in the
heart-beats! Why need it ever end? Why in
tenderest sympathy should they two not row on

forever? He had sadly called himself a poor
boatman, but was he not eminently superior to
any one she had ever, ever known? A little cot-
tage nestled among the trees on the shore of
that blessed lake, and that almost too tender,
almost too sensitive heart to—but let us throw
the veil of charity over the remainder of her
maiden meditation.

It was impossible for Tony not to compre-
hend what Binder's eyes were saying, asking,
urgently pleading. For many days he had persistently endeavored to gain a smile or friendly
glance from her. As she now stared over his
head or far out on the water, and forced herself
to keep the contempt out of her face, that Miss
Aurelia, smiling blissfully and pulling bravely
with all her strength, might not see, a sudden
and, to her, remarkable thought leaped up fresh-
ly in her perturbed brain. She repulsed it with
a shudder. It reappeared, bold and tenacious.
But Eduard? What would he say? "Never
mind. Knowing my duty—I can make him all
right afterwards." She was silent and abstracted the whole way home.

When they reached the landing she accepted
Binder's assistance for the first time, and, draw-
ing her breath hard and nerving herself as if to

touch a reptile, when he squeezed her hand, she,
Tony Zschorcher, squeezed his in return.

That evening she wrote to Eduard. After
reading the letter she tore it into many long
strips, and burned them, one by one, in her can-
dle. "Knowing my duty—" she murmured,
softly; "the best of men are queer." Some day I
will tell him—with my voice—not with written
words." Still, she was glad that she had written
the letter, for it had laid the situation clearly
before her, and exposed the enemy's weak points.
Going across to Miss Aurelia, that lady she discovered was also writing, apparently the first
draft of something important. Her manuscript
consisted chiefly of erasures, and the English-
German lexicon was lying open close at hand.

Tony asked permission to go out, which Miss
Aurelia, hustling her papers confusedly together, gave with precipitation. The maid, with her
demure, respectful air, passed out of the room;
but as the door closed her quiet face grew distressed and frightened. "There's not a moment to lose — oh, dear — oh, dear!" Smiling
again, as if life to her were purest balm, she
sought the servants' hall, and her friend, the
great High-Dudgeon.

"Oh," she began, sweetly, "would you please

be so kind? Suppose, General High-Dudgeon, that you wished your sister in England to come to you, how would you telegraph that in your English?"

"I should say, 'Emmeline, come direkly,' or words to that effect."

"Would you please write it for me?"

"That and more, for you," responded the great man, gallantly. "Must you telegraph to England? Emmeline, you know, would not be necessary unless the party's name was Emmeline."

"No, I must not telegraph to England or to Emmeline. But it does seem a shame to neglect opportunities such as I have at present to learn really superior English. All you gentlemen speak French so easily that I get on very well. Still, it would be an advantage to me to know English, and I never felt it more than at this very moment. It's a great language, your English."

"Well, that's true," he admitted, much gratified, and accepting her praise as if he were the sole originator and proprietor of the English tongue. "Shall I write some more for you, Miss Vanderpool?"

"To-morrow, thanks, Major-general High-Dudgeon," said Tony, escaping as fast as possible.

She now went straight to the telegraph office and carefully wrote a message, hesitating slightly at the signature. "Knowing my duty, it's too late to stop for trifles," she concluded, and signed her despatch with a bold "A."

Her next task was more difficult, and she turned red and white by turns as she advanced to it. On the pier some boys were playing a species of leap-frog. She called one of them.

"Do you know Fritz Binder?" she asked.

He grinned assent.

"Do you know where he is likely to be at this time?"

"Likely to be a-drinkin' beer."

"Will you find him, and give him this? And here's something for you."

Binder, in the midst of a convivial circle of men, pipes, and beer-mugs, sprang up joyfully, uttering the German equivalent of "By thunder!" Upon the paper the urchin had given him was written, "The park. Last walk. Third tree. *Now.* T."

On wings of hope he flew to the trysting-place.

A little figure in a waterproof and muffled in much veil was awaiting him.

"Oh," stammered the hero of a thousand

rowing-parties, the ideal of boarding-schools,
suddenly growing shy, awkward, and happy, "I
never expected this, never—of you!"

"Nor I either," muttered Tony, with a groan
of exasperation.

"You see, you were always so frosty and so
queer."

"Was I?" gasped Tony, hoarsely, the vials of
her wrath about to empty themselves upon
him.   There was a choking sensation in her
throat, and she had been nursing her ire and
contempt so long that now, at the critical moment, she could find no words.

"I've rowed on this lake ten years," continued the deluded young man, "and I've never
seen anything like you, and that's why I couldn't
keep my eyes off of you," coming a little nearer
and attempting to take her hand.

"Let me alone!" she exclaimed, fiercely.

"Why, Tony!"

"Don't Tony me!"

Binder had had a large experience with the
fair sex, and from these symptoms, on the part
of a young woman who had herself proposed a
rendezvous, he not unreasonably concluded that
she was jealous.

"Come—come now," he murmured, coaxing-

ly. His voice was eager and sincere. By the
dim park light she saw before her a good-looking young man in a rough coat and an unro-
mantic hat. She shrank as much as possible into
the shadow.

"Fritz Binder," she began, "Fritz Binder—
Fritz Binder, you—you ought to be ashamed of
yourself!"

"Tony, I do want to please you, awfully!
You know I do. You're mad, and no wonder,
because she and I are going to meet in the
woods to-morrow. But can I help it if she says
she wants to see me in the leafy grove? I'm
not a swan; I can show on land," stretching his strong, straight legs with a conscious
laugh.

Tony clung spasmodically to the tree and
thought that she should die.

"Too mad to speak? Well, I'm sorry. But,
honest now, could I know you'd care? And if
a lady tells a man to meet her in the woods, he
goes, doesn't he? She says she has something
to tell me—me alone. Well, I don't suppose it
will hurt me much. And if it pleases her,"
laughing heartily, "what's the odds? She isn't
the first woman that ever made a fool of herself. She won't be the last."

"The woods," repeated Tony, mechanically. "What woods?"

"You know very well, the woods beyond the villas. Don't try to fool me, you little witch. You've heard her whispering at me for days. But what's the use of wasting time about her. See here, Tony, don't play off. When a girl like you meets a man at night in this way, she's in earnest. You are in earnest, Tony?"

"Yes, I'm in earnest," she groaned.

"There, now, that's something like," he went on, cheerfully. "And I'm in earnest. I mean it as honest as ever a man did. And I won't go near the woods and that silly, scraggy old maid. It was only a lark, you know, and her money is handsome, if she isn't."

In Tony's ordinarily clear head the wildest confusion prevailed. Plans and counter-plans, indignation and astonishment, ran riot.

"Tony, don't be so queer. Be a little friendly, can't you? Haven't you a word to say to me?"

"To-morrow," she answered, with a violent effort.

"To-morrow?" he questioned, joyfully.

"Yes. I shall have something to say to you to-morrow."

"Where? Here?"

"No. In the woods."

"Oh," he laughed, "instead of the other one?"

"Yes, instead of the other one."

"But hadn't we better say somewhere else? There might be a collision."

"No. Nowhere else. Only in those woods."

"Whew! How jealous the little thing is," he thought, complacently.

"Well, well, as you like," he said, in a soothing tone. "Only take care of her."

"Yes. I'll take care of her. Trust me for that," she replied, in her strange, stifled voice.

"What, are you going?"

"Yes, I am."

"And won't even give me your hand?"

She darted off two or three steps and paused.

"You—wait until to-morrow, Fritz Binder!" she remarked, with extraordinary emphasis, and ran rapidly away.

Binder returned to his friends and indulged in sanguine reflections.

"She was only trying to punish me. I like a girl with spirit. The neat, pert, pretty, wide-awake little thing. And I shouldn't be surprised if her savings were considerable. We must make the old one give us her blessing, and fork over."

CHAPTER IX.

TONY WINS.

"I SHALL not need those things to-day, Tony," said Miss Aurelia, with a vivid blush.

Tony, as usual after lunch, had laid the boating-costume out, and the rowing gloves, and the sailor hat with the anchors.

"Why should I feel embarrassed?" thought Miss Aurelia. "Tony will soon know all."

"I am going to take a stroll in the woods," she announced, with a vain attempt at composure. "I will wear the grenadine, Tony, and the pretty little tulle hat."

Tony, with alacrity, made the requisite changes in her dispositions.

"Shall I take parasols or umbrellas?" she asked, innocently. "Umbrellas, perhaps. The weather is uncertain."

"I did not say that you were to come," stammered Miss Aurelia, with another painful blush.

"Oh, will the gracious fräulein walk in the woods quite alone? Will that be safe?"

"I'm not afraid," replied Miss Aurelia, ashamed of her equivocation, yet dwelling with pride upon the manly strength which would support and protect her.

"But am I not to meet the gracious fräulein somewhere to walk home with her?"

Miss Aurelia looked at her reflectively.

Why not? Everything would be settled then. He would have read what she had written, the outpouring of her deepest and truest sentiments. How fortunate that she had proposed the woods. There, in leafy solitude, amid the song of birds, he would not hesitate to declare himself. Would he deem her unmaidenly? Ah, no! Already he had said so very much in eloquent sighs and glances, in vague yet unmistakable hints. She did hope her German was clear enough. She had at least taken the greatest pains and written it three times. The wood was, indeed, necessary. How could she give the precious missive to him in the boat? How could he read it there? But Tony was waiting for her answer.

"Well, yes, Tony. I don't mind your coming after I am through with my walk. I prefer to

be undisturbed until five," she faltered. "I am
going at four. You might leave the hotel at
five, Tony."

"At five," Tony repeated, dutifully. "And
where?"

Tony was now quite pale, and watched her
mistress's uncertain features closely.

"I cannot have her meet him," reasoned
the lady. "He will be so rapturous, so agitated."

"Tony," she said, "you know the broad mid-
dle path. Well, you go down that as far as the
stone, and then turn to the right—the right,
you understand, Tony."   ·

"The right, gracious fräulein."

"At five or a little later, and go to the right,
Tony, and wait by that tallest pine."

"At five, to the right, and wait by the pine."

"And you may go now, Tony. I do not need
you. I have something to do. Everything is
quite ready, thanks," she said, hurriedly, longing to prepare herself once more for the coming
interview, which she had rehearsed a score of
times, picturing herself gently alluring, yet perfectly discreet—in short, all that a woman ought
to be, whose lover of humble station is con-
sumed by the passion he dares not reveal.

There was that princess who proposed to a doctor. It seemed to Miss Aurelia her case was very similar. To be sure, she was not a princess. But Fritz was certainly infinitely more fascinating than any doctor could possibly be. Then, to propose fairly and squarely was far from her intentions. She was merely going to delicately give him to understand that—

"Tony, why are you waiting?"

"There is something I would like to beg of the gracious fräulein," said the girl, softly, regarding her mistress with a singular expression which that lady was far too excited to observe. Affection, distress, pity, and something like a prayer for pardon were portrayed on the little maid's face.

"If the gracious fräulein should hear voices or anything, will she please stand perfectly still and listen, before she goes on?"

Tony was very pale indeed.

"How absurd, Tony! Those woods are so peaceful."

"Yes—but sometimes there are people there one wouldn't like to meet. I should feel so much happier," she pleaded, "if the gracious fräulein would only promise me this."

"Well, then, I promise. Why not?"

"To stand perfectly still and listen? It is a promise?"

"Yes, yes. But go now, Tony, please."

Before Miss Aurelia prepared to start, Tony was walking rapidly towards the woods. "If things only work right!" she sighed, throwing a half-frightened look back at the hotel windows. Reaching the stone in the broad path, she murmured, "To the right and wait by the pine," then unhesitatingly turned to the left, and waited by an oak, where Miss Aurelia used to come to read, in the old days before she had discovered Fritz Binder.

"If he doesn't come I could choke him," she muttered. Presently she heard a footfall on the soft turf and the breaking of little twigs.

"Thank Heaven, it's Binder."

On he came, smiling, complacent.

"Tony," he cried, stretching out his arms playfully, "give me a kiss to make up for last night."

"You stand where you are and keep your distance. First of all, you must answer some questions."

"All right," returned Binder, indulgently, "only don't try a fellow's patience too long."

It seemed to Tony's sharpened senses that

there was already a rustling in the undergrowth
not far off, and from the direction in which she
had come.

"Stand more to the right," she commanded,
hastily, "so—profile against the path."

"Are you going to take my photograph?"
laughed Binder.

"Don't move," said Tony, sternly. "Answer
me, and fast."

"Oh, I'll answer fast enough. I want my
reward."

"And honestly?"

"And honestly. Here's my hand on it."

"Keep your hands at home!"

"For the present, since it's your whim, I
will."

"Fritz Binder," she demanded, solemnly,
"where did you get all those lies you tell in
your boat?"

She spoke louder than usual, and it was not
easy for her to keep her eyes fixed on him and
at the same time to closely watch the motions
of a figure leaning against a tree at a little distance.

Binder threw back his head and laughed im-
moderately.

"Some of them at the theatre, some of them

out of my own head," he answered at last, with great glee.

"Is there any Prince Botowski?"

"There may be for all of me, but I never saw him."

"Is there any Countess Olga?"

"There is, but I don't know her."

"Is there any schoolmistress with nine young ladies from the Rhine?" demanded his stern inquisitor.

"Yes, there is, and they all dote on me. That's no lie, or the sixty-three anchors either. Most through with your catechism?"

"How many times have you repeated that weeping-willow poem? Five hundred?"

"At least."

"And you say it backwards and forwards and zigzag and upside-down, don't you?"

"Why not?" he chuckled, triumphantly. "The foreign ladies know so little German."

"Do you know any other poem?"

"Not I. I've made heaps of money out of that one. It's a splendid investment."

"And you chose it for its length, didn't you? To keep people out in your boat—night-tariff?"

"Oh, yes. It belongs to my stock in trade. Hurry, Tony. Time's about up."

" What's all that about your heart that beats
and your cruel fate and your sleepless nights?
Is there anything particular the matter with
you?"

"No, there isn't," he declared, with a great
honest laugh. "I'm sound as a nut—heart,
stomach, and liver. But, you see, suffering
pleases. No man on the lake makes as
much money as I do. Do you suppose mere
rowing pays? It's the extras, Tony, the extras."

" What extras? Tell me everything."

" What an eager little thing you are! Well,
the fact is, Tony, you can hardly make it too
strong for most women. Look at them boldly,
roll up your eyes at them, and they may say you
are impudent, but they come again the next day.
They taught me my business themselves. When
I began, I thought only of rowing. 'What a
beautiful boy,' they said, 'with his blue blouse
and his loose collar.' And they'd look at me
and talk about me as if I was a part of the pier
or the landscape. Of course, I'd have been a
born fool if I hadn't made my blouse bluer and
my collar looser, wouldn't I, little Tony?"

"Go on, go on," she exclaimed, excitedly.

" 'What an attitude,' the ladies would say;
10

'how picturesque,' as I stood quite careless like on the landing. That was ten years ago. Well, of course, I've kept that attitude and been improving upon it ever since. The picturesque pays. I've learned to spout a few phrases and to hit my breast like anything. The boat is my theatre, and the same thing answers the purpose year after year. The women always like it. They just dote on love-making. I'm sometimes surprised that they don't get tired, for I'm awfully bored often, and mighty glad to get into these other clothes, when nothing is expected of me but to take my glass of beer like an honest man, without any nonsense. But, looking at it as business, there's nothing on the lake that pays like love-making. Don't you see, Tony?"

"Oh, yes, I see."

"But the ladies teach me; the ladies began it, bless 'em. Now, that little dodge of mine about being but a poor boatman, and my aspiration and the curse of fate and all that, why, it was a lady that showed me the whole thing. She made eyes at me and asked me if I didn't suffer. Of course, I said yes. She said she saw it and sympathized with me, and I must not despair. She knew I was a noble soul. I said that I

was. She said though but an humble boatman
my aspiration soared beyond the cold and cruel
world. I said that it did. The lake-business is
queer, but it's paying, because the ladies educate
a man in his profession. I've got a couple of
pupils. They're green and shy still, and inclined
to laugh. But they'll do bravely, as soon as I
launch them. But what has all this to do with
us, Tony? Don't let's talk shop. Let's talk of
ourselves."

Tony drew her breath, grew paler, and cast a
quick glance over her shoulder.

"What have you been trying to do with Miss
Vanderpool?"

"Nothing in particular. I've had plenty of
regular customers like her, easily pleased, you
know, and liberal. It's like fishing. Some fish
bite, some don't. My bait is always the same.
It's luck. She bites."

"Have you ever met any other lady in these
woods?" she asked, in a clear voice, throwing a
pained, pitiful glance over her shoulder.

"In these woods? Good Lord! that's the
regular thing. If ever I've had a wholesale
customer like Miss Vanderpool, it always ends
in the woods."

Tony looked as if she were suffering acute

physical pain.   High and distinct came her next
question.

"And you don't love Miss Vanderpool, don't
admire her, don't care for her at all?"

It seemed to Tony that the very trees leaned
forward to listen to his answer.

He laughed merrily.

"Do you take me for a fool? Tony, business
is business, and I say and do 'what I must,
whether women are old and scraggy or not.
But, as I'm an honest man, I never before asked
a girl to marry me, and I do ask you. I don't
know anything about you. But you please me.
You've taken hold of me. Would I marry one
of those ogling, silly fools? No, not if she was
a princess. What I like is a neat, clean, clever,
sensible, pretty little thing, with a head on her
shoulders, like you, Tony. Do you suppose
I'd marry a girl that couldn't see through me?
Speak up now, yourself. Say you like me a little,
Tony.   Come now!"

She darted back as he approached.

"Fritz Binder, in the first place, I'm proud
to say that I've been engaged to be married, for
years, to a man that lives by honest work and
not upon his looks. And in the second place,
if I had nobody at all I'd be ashamed to keep

company with such as you, trading on a low-
necked shirt-collar and love-glances and lies.
And in the third place, Miss Vanderpool has
heard every word you've said from behind that
tree, and she sends her compliments and has
amused herself very much this summer, but
doesn't require your boat any more. And, as for
me, I despise you, and so good-day to you, Fritz
Binder!"

She was gone.

Binder, open-mouthed, stared after her, and
saw her join her mistress. The situation being
unequivocal, he concluded not to face the two
irate women, but to retire at once with long
strides.

Tony found Miss Aurelia pressed as close to
a tree-trunk as its mantle of moss.

How they reached the hotel neither of them
ever knew.

Tony put her mistress to bed with a hot-water
flask at her feet.

Miss Aurelia turned her face to the wall and
spoke not a word. Tony ministered to her with
vast and silent sympathy, in nameless, tender
ways that women know.

Shivers ran down Miss Aurelia's back. Hot
tears burned her eyes. She felt weak, crushed,

helpless, and infinitely ashamed. From her station behind the tree she had seen no hero, but only a vulgar and hearty young man in respectable and ill-fitting clothes. She had listened to the exposition of his principles. They were natural enough. She could even find some excuse for him. But she did not recognize him. He was to her an utterly unknown being. Where was the hero of her one romance? Where was her boatman, her gondolier, her gallant, beautiful, high-souled, aspiring, sensitive, suffering friend? She had gazed in his deep eyes for the last time yesterday in the boat. As if sunk in the lake, he had vanished forever. This heavy, respectable-looking day-laborer had nothing in common with that tender and exquisite youth.

She would fain have visited her mortification, confusion, and bitter disappointment upon Tony, but that discreet little person was a rare combination of devotion and tact, perceived no rebuff, and persisted in regarding Miss Aurelia as ill from too much rowing. She told the doctor so; she announced it to the servants and to all inquiring friends; she said it, in fact, so often that she finally believed it herself.

In the course of the following morning Mr.

John Vanderpool made his appearance, to his niece's immoderate surprise. She was lying in bed, because it suited Tony's views to keep her there, and Miss Aurelia cared too little what became of her to remonstrate.

"Well, you do look pulled down, Aurelia, upon my word," he said, kindly, after the first greetings, patting her hand with solicitude, "and you did right to telegraph."

Miss Aurelia stared, and was about to speak, when she was emphatically pinched by Tony— the only act of positive disrespect of which she was ever guilty.

"It gave me a start, my dear girl. I took the first train, and here I am. Now, what can I do for you?"

"Take me away," she said, feebly, tears starting to her eyes.

Tony hurried him out of the room.

"But she's not able to travel," he said, anxiously.

"Oh, yes; all she needs is change of air. Now her dear uncle is here she will be better. She is only fatigued from too much rowing."

"Rowing!" exclaimed the astonished old gentleman. "Can she row?"

"Magnificently," returned Tony, with enthusiasm.

Towards evening Miss Aurelia was pronounced able to be dressed, and even to take a turn on the lake with her uncle.

"I cannot, Tony, I cannot; indeed I cannot," whispered Miss Aurelia.

Tony dressed her, cheered her, comforted her, petted her, cooed over her as if she were a baby, but to the lake she had to go.

"Mr. John Vanderpool," Tony rejoined, with cheerful significance, "is a man worth seeing. When one has a gentleman like him in the family it is well that people should know it. It prevents misunderstandings."

More dead than alive, Miss Aurelia was dragged into the boat of an old, grayheaded rower. "Tony is cruel to bring me here," she groaned, as she beheld the scene of her lost illusions. Pale, passive, speechless, she leaned back with half-closed eyes.

"Isn't it too much for her?" asked Uncle John.

"She will be better for it afterwards," replied Tony, sweetly.

Presently Mr. Vanderpool broke into a hearty laugh.

"'TAKE ME AWAY,' SHE SAID FEEBLY."

"What is that dandy boatman trying to do over there?" he inquired.

At a short distance from them, in a dainty white boat, sat two ladies, gazing enraptured upon a young man attired in a highly picturesque sailor suit. He had dropped his oars, and was beating his breast vigorously. Now he stood up, and made frantic motions, as if about to plunge into the water.

"What's the matter with him? and what a theatrical puppy he is," commented Uncle John, still laughing.

"It's only Binder," volunteered the old boatman, with a grin. "He's always a-doing that. He says the ladies like it. He does act like a fool, but he ain't one on shore."

Miss Aurelia gasped for breath.

"Row towards him," said Uncle John. "Why, Tony, you ought to have engaged him. He's as good as a circus."

"The gracious fräulein has often employed Binder," Tony rejoined, seriously. "He is amusing at first, but one tires of him."

The boats approached.

Uncle John turned his laughing, quizzical face broadly upon Fritz Binder.

"He is telling about a monster who hates

women and roses," Tony calmly explained to
Mr. Vanderpool. "I know by the gestures.
Now he says that he loves, madly, yet how re-
spectfully."

"Ah, gracious fräulein," she whispered, im-
ploringly, "if you would only look happy; if
you would only sit up, and laugh straight in his
face; dear fräulein, just once, *now!*"

Inspired by her eagerness, Miss Aurelia
straightened herself, and accomplished a smile
which, if not characterized by perfect sponta-
neity, was, at least, a perceptible exercise of the
facial muscles, such as society often demands of
us; and, as the boats passed each other, Binder
saw three laughing faces surveying him; four,
in fact, for no boatman on the lake ever met
him without a knowing grin.

He stared an instant in surprise at the stout,
elderly cavalier, then, swinging his blue cap,
smiled back frankly and unabashed, the strong
sunlight shining on his handsome brown hair
and bare throat. He looked hard at Tony, con-
flicting emotions struggling in his face, but a
merry parting glance won, and, with a shrug of
his shoulders, equivalent to "After all, business
is business," he resumed the duties of his profession.

"Handsome young rogue," said Uncle John, "and enjoys life vastly. I wish I had his waist."

"His waist is a very different thing in his other clothes," returned Tony, with composure.

"Tony," said Miss Aurelia, late that night, blushing, and looking very miserable, "do you think that it is my duty to—to explain; that is to say, to relate anything that has happened to my uncle?"

"Mr. John Vanderpool," returned Tony, stoutly, "no doubt has his little pleasures which he does not relate to the gracious fräulein. The gracious fräulein has the same right to keep her little pleasures to herself. After all," she added, airily, "it was the merest bagatelle!"

Miss Aurelia gave her a grateful glance, but Tony was looking unconsciously in another direction. Happily, she was not one of the women who after every event experience the gloating desire to "talk it over," and Miss Aurelia was ashamed and sore in the deepest recesses of her heart, and only silence could heal her wounds.

The next day they left Constance amid impressive adieux, which greatly astonished Uncle John. Everybody was at the door, even the wise man from the den below, and Miss Aurelia

was presented with countless bouquets and boxes
of chocolate. Mrs. High-Dudgeon stood conspicuously in sight till the very last. Mrs. Ruy-
Bric murmured lovingly in her dearest Miss
Vanderpool's ear that she would not fail to
write to her every detail of the progress of the
little church in Wales, in which she took so
deep and gratifying interest. Mr. Puggums
toddled about and gurgled to the mystified Uncle John, " Take care of her. She is truly precious. We have all loved her well. Let me
always know the sweet girl's address." " She's
a *lady !*" thundered Mrs. High-Dudgeon, in a
tone that made Uncle John jump.

Off went the omnibus, amid wavings of hand-
kerchiefs, waftings of kisses, and obsequious salaams from the crowd of waiters. Tony had
distributed the *pourboire* prudently, not lavishly, for she knew that a millionaire need
never give as a poor man must.

"Upon my word!" exclaimed Uncle John,
looking curiously from one to the other. He
had believed that he knew his niece. Miss Aurelia was silent and pale; indifferent to her triumphs, one would say.

"She has been much admired here," said
Tony, softly.

"Indeed," remarked Uncle John, and fell into a brown study.

Several times that day Tony caught him furtively casting searching glances at his niece.

They went to a place of Tony's choosing, called Herzensruh'. (This name will not be found on Cook's list.) Here, as Miss Aurelia had desired, people were kind and enjoyed themselves. Some of them had titles which would have interfered with the enjoyment of a stern and rockbound republican. But Uncle John neither bowed down to them nor paid their owners the equally flattering tribute of scathing and contemptuous disapproval. He took them simply, as they took themselves, and found them amiable companions, good whist-players, and clever at political discussions. He even privately admitted to his own conscience that had he been born a French marquis with a large estate, he might have had a sneaking fondness for his own land, language, and associations, and succumbed to the weakness of not emigrating to America.

Tony did not push the Vanderpools here. Where others were at rest she deemed struggling out of place. Everybody was kind to Miss Aurelia and admired her rowing. Uncle John was particularly impressed with this new accomplishment.

"I would never have believed it!" he exclaimed, with much respect. "You really row very well, my dear. Who ever supposed you had any muscle and 'go'?"

"I had a great deal of practice at Constance," she would reply, at first with a blush, but gradually she took an honest pride in her rowing, and enjoyed being praised for it. The Fritz-Binder episode assumed by degrees a less painful aspect, and finally imparted a certain dignity to her meditations, and a pensive air of experience to her countenance when the tender passion was under discussion.

In every respect her uncle found her improved. She looked better, he could not tell how or why. She spoke better, with more clearness and decision; no longer irritating him with her stammering repetitions.

"Aurelia's rather nice," he found himself often thinking. "Travel is improving her. She's liked too. What a fuss they made over her at Constance." Even here at Herzensruh' the ladies said, "That quiet Miss Vanderpool must be a lovely character. Her bright, clever little maid worships the ground she walks on."

One day Uncle John was watching Tony's
healthy, supple little figure moving lightly
about the room as she put things to rights, and,
struck anew with the keen look of her eyes
and her charming smile, he demanded, suddenly,

" Tony, why haven't you married ?"

" Oh, Uncle John !" remonstrated Miss Aurelia. " Don't ! Every woman has her heart-his-
tory." She sighed, and looked wise.

" Tony doesn't mind," he persisted. " Why
aren't you married, Tony ?"

" Well, sir, I might have several times, but—"

" But—"

" But you know if you set your heart on anybody that's the end of it. The others were the
right sort, and good-looking and diligent; but
there—I don't want anybody but him !" she
exclaimed, with a splendid flash of color and a
happy smile.

" What's the matter with him ?"

" Nothing, thank God."

" Does he like you ?"

" Of course," with a serene look.

" Then you're engaged ?"

" Oh, yes, surely."

" Where is he ?"

"At his work, in a little town in the Suabian Oberland."

"What is he?"

"A master-builder. Oh, he's educated. He can talk with anybody about styles," she added, proudly. "One look at a building, and he can tell you all about it—Gothic, Renaissance, everything."

"How long have you been engaged?" demanded Uncle John.

Tony's bright, courageous face looked at him cheerily.

"Eleven years," she said.

"Here—here—is the German Fatherland!" he muttered. "But why in the dickens don't you marry?"

She hesitated.

"We shall—some day, when we have saved something."

"Jacob served fourteen years for Rachel."

"In Germany Rachel serves too," rejoined Tony, brightly.

"But why haven't you saved your earnings? You have good wages."

"You see, sir, there are the parents."

"Whose parents?"

"My parents."

"Are they feeble?"

"Happily, no. They are strong and able-bodied."

"Then, Tony, what do you mean?"

"Oh," she said, distressed, "I'm not bound to work for them. They don't ask, but if I don't give it makes me unhappy. I can't bear cold looks or the door closed on me a Sunday afternoon. It isn't the right kind of a home where there's no peace. I'd do anything for peace. And so it goes year after year. I might have had three thousand mark in the bank if it weren't for my father. The mother—it's not her fault, but, of course, when he sulks she gives way, and it's no home to come back to, so I think, 'Well, they may have it this time.'"

"How old is your father?" asked Uncle John, walking rapidly up and down the room.

"Father's forty-eight, and well and strong, and has his trade. He's not my real father."

"Where is your real father?" Mr. Vanderpool asked, much puzzled.

She hesitated.

"Is he dead?"

"I never had any," she answered, very gently.

"Ah!" said Uncle John; and thought, "Poor little girl, with your finely cut face, and your

11

brain and nerve and race and sensitiveness and
mastery of us all—this is the problem I have
unconsciously been studying; no father!"

"Tony," he began, peremptorily, "you mean
to say that you have been supporting for years
an able-bodied man who isn't even of your own
blood?"

"Since I was twelve years old I have helped
—yes."

"And for what earthly reason, I should like
to inquire?"

"He is a respectable man," she said, softly,
"and he married my mother when I was a little
baby. My mother is good and patient and
faithful—the best of women; but every man
wouldn't have done what he did. I don't know
as it's unnatural that he should expect me to do
something for him. He is so very respectable.
His reputation is excellent. Of course, it was
always a trial to him that I was there." With
a pretty, deprecating look at Miss Aurelia, "I
am very sorry," she added. "These things
aren't pleasant, but they are in the world. They
are true."

"God bless my soul, yes," ejaculated Uncle
John. After a pause, "See here, Tony," he
began, "have you never tried to stop this black-
mail business?"

"Oh, yes. That's why I came away from home. Once I had a dressmaking shop. I've learned my trade thoroughly. I was doing well, very well. But I couldn't keep anything. It all went. It will be better some day," she said, bravely.

"Does the man drink?"

"Oh, no. He is most respectable, as I have said. He is very pleasant with me, too, when all goes well. The mother is glad when we all go out together."

"Tony, my girl, it's a relief to me to be able to tell you that you are a little fool. You have struck me as so supernaturally clever, so far beyond anybody's years, so happy and gentle and cheery and good, such a paragon, in fact, that you made me rather uncomfortable. Now that I know that you are a little fool I feel better."

Mr. Vanderpool was flourishing his handkerchief about his nose and eyes in a singular manner.

Tony laughed brightly.

"You need a bit of sound advice, you and your Jacob."

"Eduard," she corrected prettily, and as if she loved the name.

"You two ought to marry and done with it,

and start fresh somewhere else. Eleven years! Merciful powers!"

"It's I that won't go to him with empty pockets. He would take me without a penny. But his parents are very respectable. They have the right to look high." She sighed, but quickly smiled again. "He will wait," she said.

"Have you never thought of going far away with him?"

"Oh, yes. But it's such a step."

"It's more than a step, it's a voyage. You send for Jacob, and let me have a talk with him. I may want to engage a master-builder myself—one that knows Gothic from Renaissance. I think you'd better leave all these very respectable old parties. And I presume you could look after Miss Vanderpool just the same, couldn't you? Aurelia, they might have a couple of rooms in the gardener's house, I should think. Once in America, Tony, you could easily bring your people to terms, and help them, too, very decently if you should wish."

"America!" exclaimed Tony, rosy with delight. "Oh, sir—"

"Oh, Tony! oh, Uncle John! What a beautiful and perfect plan!"

"You send for Jacob," he repeated, as he left the room.

"Knowing my duty—I will."

"Tony," Miss Aurelia began, "I am glad, too, that you have been foolish. It was good and generous, but foolish, very. Everybody is foolish once," she said, with a sigh, and her newly-acquired look of romantic reminiscence; "but some more than others. Tony, there is something—we have never spoken of it; I never could—but I have often wished to ask you since—since that peculiar and unfortunate experience on the Lake of Constance, when—"

"Since the gracious fräulein chose to learn to row," suggested Tony, serenely.

"Yes, since I chose to learn to row. It is this, Tony. Do you, or do you not, know right from left?"

"When the gracious fräulein explains I seem to understand," began Tony, casting down her eyes.

Miss Aurelia shook her head incredulously.

"That day—that dreadful day, Tony—there was enough that I understood too well; but there was much I could not understand. I told you the right path, and you had time to think and choose, and yet you went to the left. How

much was accident, Tony? How much did you
know?"

Tony hesitated an instant. Her eyes sparkled.

"Gracious fräulein," she answered, "I've
knocked about this world more than a dear,
good, innocent lady can ever imagine, and this
much I've learned. Things are right or left according as one stands. The path I took was
the right path—coming home!"

Miss Aurelia looked at her in gentle per-
plexity.

"Ah, Tony, I fear that you are a sad rogue."

The little maid returned her gaze with a benevolent and humorous smile.

"Knowing my duty, gracious fräulein — I
am."

THE END.